Emily Harvale lives in
although she would prefer to live in
Alps ... or Canada ... or anywhere that has
several months of snow. Emily loves snow
almost as much as she loves Christmas.

Having worked in the City (London) for several
years, Emily returned to her home town of
Hastings where she spends her days writing ...
and wondering if it will ever snow.

You can contact her via her website, Twitter,
Facebook or Instagram.

There is also a Facebook group where fans can
chat with Emily about her books, her writing
day and life in general. Details can be found on
Emily's website.

Author contacts:
www.emilyharvale.com
www.twitter.com/emilyharvale
www.facebook.com/emilyharvalewriter
www.instagram.com/emilyharvale

***

Scan the code above to see all Emily's books on Amazon

Also by this author

The Golf Widows' Club
Sailing Solo
Carole Singer's Christmas
Christmas Wishes
A Slippery Slope
The Perfect Christmas Plan
Be Mine
It Takes Two
Bells and Bows on Mistletoe Row

Lizzie Marshall series:
Highland Fling – book 1
Lizzie Marshall's Wedding – book 2

The Goldebury Bay series:
Ninety Days of Summer – book 1
Ninety Steps to Summerhill – book 2
Ninety Days to Christmas – book 3

The Hideaway Down series:
A Christmas Hideaway – book 1
Catch A Falling Star – book 2
Walking on Sunshine – book 3
Dancing in the Rain – book 4

Hall's Cross series
Deck the Halls – book 1
The Starlight Ball – book 2

Michaelmas Bay series
Christmas Secrets in Snowflake Cove – book 1
Blame it on the Moonlight – book 2

ISBN 978-1-909917-65-1

Published by Crescent Gate Publishing

Print edition published worldwide 2020
E-edition published worldwide 2020

Editor Christina Harkness

Cover design by JR and Emily Harvale

Emily Harvale

Christmas at Aunt Elsie's

CRESCENT GATE PUBLISHING

To all the wonderful volunteers and charitable organisations who help to keep our beaches clean and who work so hard to save the creatures who live in our seas, especially those who do such sterling work to try to save seahorses. The gentle seahorses need all the help they can get.

Map of Seahorse Harbour

There's an interactive map, with more details,
on my website: www.emilyharvale.com

One

I was beginning to think this was a huge mistake as I drove down the steep hill leading into Seahorse Harbour. I'd been making a lot of mistakes over the past three years, so that was nothing new. But seeing the line of funeral cars, the gleaming black funeral coach and the six horses, their ebony coats shining in the cold December air and their glossy manes teased by the biting afternoon breeze, really gave me the creeps.

What if I'd come too late? What if this was Aunt Elsie's funeral?

I don't know why I thought that, but I did, and I hoped to God I hadn't just lost Aunt Elsie. Christmas was already looking bleak. Her being dead would make it utterly miserable.

Not that I really knew her. I think I'd only met her a handful of times in my life. But she was the only living connection to my parents and although she wasn't related to me by blood, but by marriage, she was still family. And right at that moment, I really needed family.

But I hadn't told my aunt I planned to visit. In fact, I hadn't really *planned* my visit at all. It was a spur-of-the moment decision. And one I was beginning to think I may have reason to regret, as I drove right past the turning for Rock Road, where the Sunrise Bed & Breakfast was situated. The journey had already been a pain in the proverbial with roadworks, diversions, delays and endless queues of traffic. Perhaps the Universe was trying to tell me something. Like go home and don't continue on to Seahorse Harbour. So when I missed the turning, I wondered if that was yet another sign.

I had been so busy taking in the gorgeous vista of the seahorse-shaped cliffs to my left, set against a gun metal grey sky and a flat-calm, steely grey sea, where the sun hung low in a pillow of purple, pink and red clouds, that I hadn't heard my sat-nav telling me to take the next turning on the right. I not only missed that one but also the next road where I could've turned around, so after telling me I was stupid, my sat-nav calculated an alternative route.

Well, it didn't actually call me stupid, but I always thought there was a rather judgemental tone to her voice, as if she were saying, 'Why do you bother asking me for directions? You never listen and you always end up having to double back.'

I was looking for somewhere to do just that when a sizeable formation of heavy-looking clouds swept down from the north, across the fields to my right and released a shower of thick, fluffy-looking snowflakes. Great. Snow. That was all I needed.

Seeing those cars parked outside the church only emphasized my feeling of unease ... and meant I also missed the next turning on the right – Meadow Lane. Now, my rather irritating sat-nav informed me I'd have to drive right around the church. And I realised I'd also have to avoid running down anyone in the crowd of people crossing the road to attend this funeral.

But it couldn't be Aunt Elsie's funeral, could it? She couldn't possibly have dropped dead in the last few days.

Could she?

Her Christmas card and round robin letter had only plopped onto my door mat two days before.

Although that didn't mean anything. Dad had dropped dead one sunny Sunday, January morning three years ago just one month after Mum had succumbed to the pancreatic cancer that had shocked us all with its sudden arrival, its aggression, and its determination to take her from us as quickly as possible. Both Dad and I were devastated, but we'd supported each other through those first few weeks and I had started to hope that we'd be okay – eventually ... until that Sunday morning when his coffee cup had slipped from his hands, along with his smile of, 'Good morning, sweetheart', and seconds later he'd followed the cup to the floor.

He didn't smash into pieces like the cup, but I immediately knew he was dead. That didn't stop me from giving him mouth to mouth and frantically pumping his heart in a futile attempt to bring him back to me. I was more of an optimist in those days. I even thought Mum would beat her cancer. Life taught me I couldn't be more wrong. About lots of things.

Until three years ago I'd had a pretty perfect life. Mum and Dad were the best parents in the world. They adored me and supported me and all my, sometimes questionable, choices.

We lived in a sprawling but ramshackle Victorian villa which Dad was always 'doing up' but never seemed to finish. He converted the lower ground floor into a flat for me, so that I could have my own space and privacy but could still pop upstairs to spend time with my parents and they could pop down to visit with me. They gave me the key to my very own front door on my twenty-first birthday.

Lower ground floor sounds like a cellar, doesn't it? But it was far from that. As with many Victorian homes, the ground floor was actually raised and reached by a staggered flight of stone steps: five steps and then a sort of terrace area followed by five more steps to the impressive front door. That meant the lower ground was only a few feet – and a flight of eight stone steps – down from the front garden. It had its own separate entrance – used by servants in the era it was built – and its own, not quite as impressive, front door.

I loved living in that flat, but when Mum and Dad passed away it didn't feel the same and after a matter of months, I'd had to sell the house because I couldn't afford the upkeep. They had left me some money but they'd never been rich, and I've always been hopeless with finances, so I had no savings of my own. I considered keeping the flat and selling the upper part, but no one seemed interested, so in the end I'd had to sell it all as one. I think I got a good price for it, considering all the work it needed, and I used the proceeds to buy a little cottage in the country and have some cash in the bank for a rainy day. I'd always loved the idea of living in rural splendour. Well, maybe not splendour – more like cosy quaintness.

The reality of muddy lanes, no street lights, no mains gas, only oil, and isolation was a real eye-opener. And it seemed to rain a lot – both figuratively and literally.

Who knew that a cottage could cost as much to repair and maintain as a large, sprawling house? At least my cottage did. Or that when it did actually rain, owning a cottage right beside a stream was not as idyllic as it had at first seemed, particularly when the stream became a raging torrent intent on establishing a new tributary directly through my cottage.

And I had no idea that thatched roofs were home to several living creatures, none of which I particularly wanted to get to know.

I lost a lot of money when I eventually managed to sell it and return to civilisation.

Now I had a rented flat. Being a property owner had not worked out well for me, and besides, I had expected my long-term boyfriend, Clark to ask me to move in with him any day.

Except he didn't.

He abruptly ended our relationship instead.

On top of that, I'd lost my job. Although I should've left Barratt, Rose & Corne long before. I'd never wanted to work for a firm of undertakers and I'm still not sure how I had come to do so. I blame it on a series of mistakes.

I wasn't entirely thinking rationally after Mum and Dad passed away and, having been made redundant the week before Mum's diagnosis, I had no money coming in. Then, when I sold the house and bought the country cottage, I foolishly thought I could live cheaply and self-sufficiently off the land and with the remaining sale proceeds. Take it from me, it may look like the perfect lifestyle and fairly easy on all those TV shows but the reality is completely different. Especially if you're living on your own and really don't know one end of a chicken from the other. By the time I realised country life probably wasn't for me, I'd been without a proper job for a year.

So when a friend of my late Dad, told me that a friend of his needed an office manager, I hadn't asked what type of office I'd have to manage. I got the job after one short telephone interview. It seems there are some jobs no one wants.

The people were lovely, don't misunderstand me. But the premises were as gloomy as my cottage, and listening to funeral music day in and day out, did nothing to lighten my mood. Seeing clients in tears each day didn't help. I'd been more than a little depressed when I took the job. By the time I lost it last week, I was ... well, let's just say that I was seriously close to needing the services of Barratt, Rose & Corne, myself.

The six large, beautiful horses neighed as I slowly drove past them, their clouds of warm breath mingling with the dancing snowflakes in the chilly air. I couldn't believe how many people were queuing to get into the quaint, Norman church.

It sat in what looked like the centre of the

village on a little 'island' of green, with a massive and rather imposing ancient oak tree with a bright yellow bench beneath it. I could imagine that bench was the perfect place to sit and while away an hour or so on a hot, summer day. Today, you'd be likely to freeze on the spot. Although the myriad, white lights, sparkling in the oak tree made me instantly think how romantic it would be to sit on that bench in this snow shower with Clark.

No. Not with Clark. I must forget Clark. Clark was history. Clark was in the French Alps, skiing with his friends. Clark was now my ex.

I drove around the island and watched all the people dressed in the sombre black you rarely saw at funerals these days. Most of the clients using Barratt, Rose & Corne seemed to go for the 'Let's celebrate our dearly departed's life, and wear bright colours to show how thankful we are to have had them in our lives', not, 'Let's wear black from head to toe to show how bereft we are at having lost the ones we love'. I wore black to Mum and Dad's funerals, but I wish I'd worn my usual, bright and cheerful clothes. I know that seems foolish. The colour of my clothes wouldn't have changed the way I felt.

I circled the church and read the name, St Mary Star of the Sea on a board to one side of the lychgate entrance. That had a certain ring to it and despite the situation I caught myself smiling just a little – until I spotted the tiny graveyard at the rear of the church. I hadn't noticed that on my way down the hill because I was so busy looking at the line of cars and the coach and horses.

But at least the small, wooden building attached to this side of the church, which I assumed was the church hall, looked bright and festive. Strings of multi-coloured lantern-shaped lights hung from the guttering right the way around in a somewhat higgledy-piggledy fashion. A wreath the size of a car tyre sat proudly on the bright red door and to one side of that stood a plump, dark green pine, pear-shaped Christmas tree, the tip of which tilted a fraction to one side beneath the weight of a sparkling, golden star.

To the other side of the red door, a nativity scene sheltered beneath a smaller replica of the lychgate. Mary, Joseph, the baby Jesus and a host of plastic animals looked warm and cosy in spite of the snow swirling all about. Although I'm not sure a polar bear or a penguin made it to the *real* event, but the donkey and the cow seemed right at home.

Seeing all that cheered me up, but I was still wondering whose funeral it was as I drove back up Seahorse Cliffs road towards the Sunrise Bed & Breakfast. Perhaps the owner of the B&B would know who was being laid to rest. From the two conversations we'd exchanged, I got the impression that Lilith Shoe seemed to know everything about the village and its residents, and was more than happy to share the information.

'Now I'm not one to gossip,' she'd said, the first time we spoke – and then proceeded to do just that. Not that I knew who she was talking about, but it was clear that Lilith was not the sort of person you would want to tell your secrets to. Not if you wanted them kept secret.

Luckily, I had no secrets. I was an open book, so Mum and Dad had always said when they smiled and hugged me close.

'I can always tell what you're thinking and feeling, sweetheart,' Mum repeatedly told me. 'You have such an expressive face and your emotions light up your eyes, whether good or bad.'

Strangely though, that's not what my ex-boyfriend, Clark thought. On the day he told me he was 'going to find himself' and that 'our relationship had run its course', he also said that he never knew what I wanted and that he wasn't a mind-reader, so how was he supposed to know that I was hoping he would ask me to move in with him.

The fact that I'd hinted about it several times, and not in a subtle manner, had clearly gone right over his head.

'I thought you weren't particularly

interested in marriage and kids and stuff,' he'd said.

I wasn't. Particularly. But that didn't mean I didn't want those things one day. Perhaps. With the right man.

'I wasn't suggesting we should rush down the aisle,' I'd told him. 'All I was hoping was that we could spend more time together. As a couple. Under the same roof.'

He had given me a blank look, shrugged and said that if he had known that's what I was hoping, he would've told me long ago that he didn't see the same future for us.

I've never been good at relationships, which is weird bearing in mind Mum and Dad had the perfect marriage. They had met when they were five, been friends, fallen in love in their teens, wed in their early twenties, and were married for fifty-five years. I'd been with Clark for two years, and at thirty-three, that was the longest relationship I'd ever had.

I really thought we would spend the rest of our lives together until that fateful day when he told me he needed to 'find himself'. But quite how spending three weeks skiing in the French Alps with his mates would help him 'find himself' was still beyond my comprehension. And why had he been dating me for the last two years if he had no intention of taking our relationship further?

When I asked him that, he'd merely

shrugged again and said, 'We had fun, didn't we?'

I think what he was actually telling me was that now he wanted to have some fun with someone else.

I knew it wouldn't take him long to find a replacement. Clark's a good-looking guy. But even I was surprised to see he seemed to have obtained another girlfriend just a few days after we had broken up. He'd only been in the French Alps for three days and already his social media was crammed full of photos of him and a rather beautiful blonde.

Not that I checked his social media much. Only once or twice. Okay, possibly a few more times than that. But it wasn't as if I was stalking him or anything. And I didn't comment on any of his fun-filled posts, no matter how tempted I might have been to do so. I played it cool.

Which reminded me that I must find my phone. I wasn't sure where, exactly, it went when I threw it onto the back seat after seeing the last update he'd posted, as I'd waited for the lights to change at a particularly busy junction.

Bastard! How could he be having so much fun without me? Wasn't he even a little bit sad that our relationship was over?

Clark was also the reason I no longer had a job. The rest of the partners were happy to keep me on, but Clark Corne, the youngest partner in the business, having taken over from his now retired dad, felt it might be better if I found a position elsewhere. Now that we were no longer dating.

He was right, of course, although I didn't think that at the time. It would be no fun walking into that building and remembering all the times we'd had sex in there. Possibly a little inappropriate, but Clark was always keen when it came to sex. We'd made love in every room, office and store cupboard in the place, which had once been a three-storey, Edwardian home of ample proportions but was now a rather old and bad, conversion, with offices exactly as they were when they were installed in the 1970s refurbishment.

I told Clark – and everyone else in the building at the time, due to my slightly raised and possibly a little hysterical tone – that he could take his job and shove it up his ... Well, I'm sure you don't need me to tell you where.

I'm still cringing at my behaviour that day, just one week ago. Not only did I scream like a demented woman, I also ran my hands over his desk and knocked everything to the floor. And then I stamped on it all. Several times.

That wasn't the sort of thing I would normally do. I think I must've had a mini-breakdown or something. I really do. Although it might have been due to the second bottle of wine I'd drunk at lunch after Clark had broken his devastating news and left me sitting in the restaurant, my mouth opening and closing unable to manage even one syllable in reply. He also left me with the lunch bill, so I'd returned to the office to tell him what a pig he was ... and a few more things besides.

Barratt, Rose & Corne didn't have security guards. It wasn't really the sort of place where people usually caused trouble ... or stole things, but I can tell you that Roger Barratt and Kenneth Rose are really very strong.

I regret giving Kenneth that black eye. I'm not a violent person. Truly, I'm not. He simply got in the way of my somewhat heated ranting and gesticulations.

I suppose I'm lucky they didn't call the police. And it was very kind of them to send my personal belongings on to me. And to pay me for the month. And not to deduct anything from my severance pay to cover the cost of the damage I'd caused.

A loud snore and the slap of flapping ears made me glance over my shoulder.

'You're awake now are you, gorgeous? You've slept the entire way here. Even my phone hitting you on your tail didn't wake you. Welcome to Seahorse Harbour.'

A muffled bark was the reply. Merry isn't the most talkative spaniel on the planet. But she is the most beautiful. I think so anyway. And definitely, the most loyal. And now it was just me and Merry against the world. At least that's how it felt.

Actually, that's how it had felt ever since Mum and Dad died. Merry was the last Christmas present they gave me. I often think they knew something I didn't and had bought me Merry so that I wouldn't be entirely on my own. Mum had died on New Year's Eve and Dad, just four weeks later.

Oddly enough, Merry never liked Clark. The first day she met him she raised the right side of her mouth and growled at him and she'd been doing that ever since. I'd tell her, lovingly, to be nice, and she'd go and sit in her basket and nuzzle her way beneath her blanket where she'd keep her gorgeous, brown eyes fixed firmly on us, the entire time Clark was there. The minute he left, she'd dash up to me for a snuggle as if she wanted to be sure that I was okay, after which she'd either stay cuddled up with me, or return to her bed and go to sleep, happy in the knowledge that Clark was no longer around.

I never felt completely alone with Merry by my side, although this would be the first Christmas that it would be just Merry and me. Clark and I had started dating the week after I joined the firm the first December after Mum and Dad had passed away, so that first Christmas, Clark and I spent in the throes of passion. This year, Merry and I would be on our own.

But we were going to see Aunt Elsie, so we wouldn't be entirely on our own this Christmas. Assuming she was happy to see us, that is. Perhaps I should've told her I was coming. Perhaps I should've thought things through and not made yet another spur-of-the moment decision.

As I mentioned earlier, Aunt Elsie was my aunt by marriage, not by blood and we'd never been close. Her late husband, Eric, who died in his early thirties, was Mum's younger brother. But Mum and Dad always said that Elsie was a truly wonderful person; she simply wasn't good at maintaining relationships. Of any sort. At least she and I had that in common.

'Elsie is a free spirit, sweetheart,' Mum would often say, with an oddly affectionate smile. As if Elsie held a very special place in Mum's heart. 'She loves us all, but she loves us from a distance. But you can be sure of one thing. If ever you need her, Elsie will be there for you.'

Mum said that several times during her brief illness, and Aunt Elsie had said almost the same thing when I'd seen her at the funerals. At Dad's funeral, she had made a point of seeking me out and telling me that I wasn't alone, that I could always count on her and that she would always be there for me. She'd even suggested I might like to go and stay with her for a while. To be honest though, I'd hardly seen her while my parents were alive and she was as good as a stranger to me.

In retrospect, perhaps that's exactly what I should've done. Instead, I'd told her I would be okay and that I needed to be on my own.

She'd made me promise to contact her if I ever needed anything but until now, other than the odd letter, and birthday and Christmas cards, I never had. She'd written to me a few times but my replies had been brief and I think she realised I wasn't really interested in building a relationship with her.

I don't know why I felt that way. She seemed kind, caring and genuinely concerned about me. But grief does strange things to us and Aunt Elsie was so full of life, so positive, so ... enthusiastic and eager to please that I just didn't want her around. I think I wanted to wallow in my melancholy and as ridiculous as it sounds, I'm not sure Aunt Elsie would have let me do that. I got the distinct impression that she was one of those annoyingly happy people who isn't fazed by anything in life.

'I know it doesn't feel like it right now,' she had said at Dad's funeral, 'but time is a great healer and life does go on. Things will get better, you'll see. And remember, Lottie. You'll always have me. We're family. I'm only a phone call away and my door is always open for you. Always. No matter what.'

I remembered those very words the day the

Christmas card and round robin letter landed on my mat.

I'm not a person who has that many friends but the ones I do have were all spending the holidays with their families. One or two of them had invited me to join them, but somehow it didn't feel right. And when I read the hand-written note Elsie had added to my letter, I knew exactly what I was going to do. I was going to spend Christmas in Seahorse Harbour and finally go and visit her. Because I really needed *family* now for some strange reason, and Aunt Elsie was the only living relative I knew.

Assuming, of course, glancing at my rear-view mirror, that Aunt Elsie wasn't in the shimmering black and gold coffin I'd just seen being removed from that magnificent coach.

No. Aunt Elsie wasn't in that coffin. I must try to be positive. That was my new mantra. I'd adopted it a couple of days ago after reading in a magazine that we attract to ourselves what we give out. So if you send out only negative emotions into the world, it'll send you back a whole lot of crap, but if you send out joy and kindness and love, the world will send you all those things right back.

I think that might be true. When Mum and Dad were alive, I was always happy and positive – even though I still wasn't good at relationships with men. Life was wonderful in almost every way. After my parents were gone, I was miserable and sad – and everything went wrong. Surely then, if I became happy and positive, things would begin to go well?

I decided to give it a try.

The fact that my washing machine ground to a rather loud and clunky halt that very same day, and then my kettle blew up the following day made me feel it wasn't working as it should, but I realised they were just late returns from my previously unhappy thoughts, so I was determined to look on the bright side of life from now on.

No matter what it threw at me, even if I had doubts and a few misgivings.

And with my loyal and devoted Merry by my side and my new, positive outlook on life, I was certain the future would be bright.

At least it couldn't get worse.

Could it?

Two

Rock Road was less than two minutes' drive from the church but by the time I pulled up outside the guest house, the roads, pavements, hedges and houses were covered in a layer of glistening white snow.

I grabbed my bright red coat, knitted blue bobble hat and matching scarf from the passenger seat and quickly threw them on, the moment I stepped out of the car. I slung my handbag over my shoulder and retrieved my case and overnight bag from the boot. Merry's poinsettia-patterned coat was on the back seat, and after finding my phone in the rear footwell, I strapped her into her coat, attached her lead and held it tight. Merry has a tendency to chase anything and everything that moves and the last thing I needed was for her to run off after something whipped up by the increasingly wintry breeze. Especially as the B&B was only across the road from Seahorse Cliffs. I had read a bit about the village online and the cliffs were more than thirty feet high in places. Seahorse Point, in particular, was dangerous. People had died jumping off there. Although why anyone would want to knowingly leap off a cliff into treacherous seas below was a mystery to me.

That said, Merry had tried to leap off a cliff once. But I'm not sure she did it knowingly. She was chasing a leaf at the time and wasn't aware of her surroundings. Thankfully, I had her on the extended lead and I somehow managed to pull her to safety just as she leapt in the air. It almost gave me a heart attack, so now I'm extra careful whenever we go within fifty feet of a cliff-edge. Not that there were any cliff edges near where we lived in Reading.

On reflection, coming to spend Christmas in a tiny village that was built on cliffs, had cliffs as most of its coastline and cliffs rising up behind the village as well as in and around it, was possibly not a good idea.

'Come on then, Merry,' I coaxed. As soon as her paws touched the ground, she bounced up and down, trying to catch snowflakes in her mouth. 'Let's go and meet Lilith Shoe. She sounds a bit like a character from a Christmas ghost story to me. I hope she doesn't look like one.'

Merry barked once in response before sneezing away a snowflake that had landed on her nose.

We walked side by side and I pressed the

doorbell, admiring the massive wreath of holly, ivy and candy canes on the deep blue painted front door. A peel of Christmas bells rang out from the musical doorbell. How jolly. Nothing frightening about that.

Seconds later, the door swung open and a beaming, buxom, ginger-haired woman, probably in her fifties, sang out 'Merry Christmas! You must be Charlotte. Oh my. You're as pretty as a picture, aren't you? I've always loved strawberry blonde hair. And this gorgeous bundle of black and white fur must be Merry. Welcome. Welcome. Welcome. Come in, come in, come in.'

Was that an Irish accent I detected? She hadn't sounded Irish when we spoke on the phone. And why was she repeating things?

She was dressed from head to toe in green and stood at about four feet eleven, I guessed; a good six inches shorter than me. I know I shouldn't say this, but she reminded me of a picture I'd seen of a leprechaun. Her face was rosy-cheeked and freckled and the tip of her nose was larger than the rest of it and turned up slightly at the end. Her eyes were large and a vivid green, the likes of which I'd never seen before and her abundant, ginger curls were styled by a clown's hairdresser, by the looks of it. She stepped aside to let us in.

'Hello and Merry Christmas to you, too. Yes, this is Merry and I'm Charlotte, but please call me Lottie. Everyone does. I can't believe it's snowing. Sorry we're so much later than I'd said we'd be. I got a bit lost despite the sat-nav, and the traffic was horrendous plus there were delays and diversions. Then I drove right past this road and the next roads too and had to turn around in the village. I was so sad to see there's a funeral taking place.'

'A funeral!' Lilith seemed shocked and shot a look at her watch as she led us towards the stairs. 'Goodness gracious. Is that the time? I must've nodded off. Oh dear me, I'm late. That'll never do. Let me show you to your room and quickly tell you where everything is. I'm afraid I'll have to dash off and leave you to it, my dear. I expected you at 2 but it's almost 3.30 unless my watch has stopped. Which it hasn't. Never mind. Follow me. First door on the right at the top of the stairs. Your room has a view of the bay. It's en suite, of course, and you'll have everything you need. There are tea, coffee and hot chocolate sachets together with milk cartons by the kettle. Help yourself. Here's the key to your room and one to the front door. Don't lose that or I'll have to charge you for the change of locks. Goodness me. I must fly. I won't be long though and we can have a good chat when I get back. I'm so sorry, my dear, but I didn't want to tell you over the phone that I'd have to leave to go to a funeral on the day you arrived. Not that I liked the woman. But I've got to go and pay my respects. The entire village will be there.'

'Er. No. Of course not. That's fine. Don't worry about us. You go. We might have a little nap ourselves. But Mrs Shoe?' She was about to dash off but she turned and smiled. 'May I ask whose funeral it is?'

Her dark ginger, grey-speckled brows shot together and she tipped her head to one side.

'Do you know anyone in Seahorse Harbour?'

'Er. A distant relative, that's all.'

The brows shot up. 'Really? You never said. Who might that be then?'

'Elspeth Morris.'

'Elsie? You're related to Elsie? Well, I never. You kept that quiet. Why aren't you staying with her then, dear?'

'We ... we don't really know one another that well and I haven't seen her for a while. I didn't want to impose.'

'Impose? Elsie wouldn't have minded in the least. You must tell me all about the connection when I get back.' She turned to go but she hesitated for a second and gave me a thoughtful look. 'Do you know the Dunns?'

'The Dunns? The name sounds familiar but I don't think so.'

'Oh well. Elsie will be at the funeral. Would you like to come with me? Or shall I just mention that you're here?'

'No! Sorry. I didn't mean to shout. But please don't mention me. I want it to be a surprise.'

'A surprise? Right you are. Oh goodness. I must be off. Make yourself at home.'

She hurried towards the stairs and I stood in the doorway of my room, not quite sure what was happening. I dropped Merry's lead and chased after her, leaning over the banisters as she raced down the stairs at the speed of light. She was very sprightly, I'll say that for her.

'You didn't say whose funeral it was,' I called after her, as I heard the front door slam. I returned to my room where Merry was busy sniffing everything. 'Oh well. At least we know it wasn't Aunt Elsie's funeral. Lilith offered to tell Elsie I was here, so my aunt clearly isn't dead.'

I breathed a sigh of relief and now that it was just me and Merry, I glanced around the room. It was as pretty in reality as it had looked on the internet.

A rectangular, cerise rug covered about half of the polished, wooden floor. Pale pink, floral curtains hung at a wide bay window and matched the bedding on a comfy-looking double bed. A built-in wardrobe and a chest of drawers took up the length of one wall and a mish-mash of prints and paintings together with the door to the en suite, took up the other. A table and two comfy-looking, cerise armchairs with plump cushions in the same pattern as the curtains and bedding, sat in the bay window, next to which was an ornate, antique radiator, painted pale pink.

I walked towards the window and admired the glorious view. I could see the sea and a few dappled rays of the setting sun, now almost completely obscured by snow clouds, from where I stood. Strange that the place should be called Sunrise B&B when the view was clearly to the west and the sunset, but that didn't matter.

The room was bright and cheerful and the radiator pumped out so much heat that I was tempted to open the window. But I didn't. Until Merry was settled I didn't want to risk her attempting to jump out of it. She'd done that once as well. Thankfully, that window had been on the ground floor.

I love her to bits but she can be a bit of a handful at times. She's definitely got an adventurous streak. Unlike me. Coming to visit my distant aunt was as adventurous as my life got these days. Possibly, ever.

I'd been on holiday and done a few exciting things, but I'd never had a real adventure. Perhaps that was something I should change? Maybe I'd do something adventurous for my thirty-fourth birthday in February.

Not that February was a month that screamed 'adventure'. It was more the type of month that whispered 'romance'. Or in my case, this coming February would sigh and say, 'Curl up in front of the fire with a hot chocolate and a good book.'

Perhaps I'd wait until the weather warmed up before thinking about adventures.

The en suite was also pink; pale pink tiles from floor to ceiling with a cerise mat beside the shower cubicle and a matching blind at the small window. Cerise bath towels and pale pink hand towels hung on a heated towel rail. At least I wouldn't suffer from cold while I stayed here.

I took off my coat and sat on the edge of the bed, flopping back and stretching out my arms. It was extremely comfortable. I was sure I would have no trouble sleeping during my stay.

Merry leapt up beside me, and while I wasn't sure that Mrs Shoe would approve of having a dog on the bed, as the woman wasn't here, she wouldn't know, would she? I'd brought Merry's bed, but I'd also brought a large fleece, in case Merry felt a little anxious on her first night in a strange place.

I got the fleece from the bag containing Merry's things and spread it out on the bed. She instantly sprawled across it, stretching out her legs and yawning as if she'd had an exceedingly busy day, and hadn't been fast asleep for the entire journey. But I couldn't really blame her. The trip had made me feel sleepy too and the warmth of the room only added to that. I'd just shut my eyes for a few minutes. The drive had taken so much longer than I'd anticipated – or than my sat-nav had informed me – and my eyes were feeling a little strained.

As I closed them and luxuriated in the quiet and cosiness of my room, I could hear a strange noise. I thought it might be the wind, as that was definitely getting stronger, but then I realised the swishing and swooshing sound was the sea lapping at the cliffs.

If that was what it sounded like when it was calm, I couldn't imagine how loud it might be when the sea was rough. I wasn't sure if I was looking forward to finding out. I was a total landlubber and the only times I'd been at the seaside were on balmy, summer days, or while on holiday in wonderfully warm places like Turkey, Greece, Egypt and the like. I don't think I'd ever seen the sea when it was wild, except on the news on TV.

Images of waves crashing over harbour walls, promenades and houses were impressive and awe-inspiring to watch but they probably weren't so fascinating when you were on the receiving end of them.

Now I was glad the Sunrise B&B was near the top of the cliffs. And far enough away from the edge so that there was no risk of the building tumbling into the sea one stormy night. I'd seen that happen on the news, too.

I got up from the bed just in time to see a spout of water shoot high in the air from what seemed to be the middle of the cliff opposite.

'That must be 'The Weeping Eye', Merry. I read about that on the internet. The sea rushes into a cave in the cliffs below and the force of the water pushes it up through an eye-shaped hole at the top of the cliff.'

I looked at Merry, eager to share the sight, but she was already sound asleep. She had moved to a more comfortable position and her head now lay on the pillow with her body stretched out on the fleece. Her tongue flopped from her half-open mouth and she snored softly, her paws twitching as she dreamt. These days it seemed, I often ended up talking to myself.

But now that I thought about it, even when I was with Clark, I'd ended up doing that. He'd be scrolling on his phone, or watching something on TV while I was chattering away. When I asked for his response, he'd merely nod, or say, 'Yeah', no matter whether it was appropriate or not.

I watched the water spout for a minute or two and then made myself a cup of hot chocolate and sat in one of the comfy chairs. I loved hot chocolate. It was Mum's favourite drink and we'd cover it with cream and grated chocolate and add a chocolate flake and often, some chocolate buttons. This hot chocolate was unadorned, so I picked up one of the little biscuits that were individually wrapped and sitting in a Christmassy bowl beside the kettle, tore off the wrapper and dunked it in my drink.

I could see quite a way down Seahorse Cliffs road from where I sat in the bay window, but I couldn't quite see the church because the road curved slightly. I could see the shops and cottages opposite the church though and the car park of what looked like a pub.

That must be The Seahorse Inn. I'd read about that too. Centuries ago it had been the haunt of smugglers. Legend had it that a tunnel led from the pub to the graveyard of the church, but no one had ever found it, despite a number of searches being made over the years.

I had also read that the owner, a man called Mikkel Meloy, had refurbished the place when he'd bought it a year or so ago, and that he also owned a restaurant and a nightclub, together with a place called The Boathouse. All of those, apart from the pub, were located on the promenade called Sea Walk.

I'd liked the sound of The Boathouse, especially as it was exactly that – a house made from an old, upturned boat, which Mikkel Meloy now rented out as a short-term holiday let. The letting information stated that it had been the home of a man called Harry Boatman who had lived there his entire life until he died at the age of one hundred. Unfortunately for me, The Boathouse was fully booked.

I'd also thought about staying at the Seahorse Harbour Holiday Park, until I realised that it meant sleeping in a mobile home. They all looked beautiful and as comfy and cosy as my current room, but listening to torrential rain pounding on what was effectively a tin roof, didn't appeal to me. And however *fixed* the things might be, they were called mobile homes for a reason. I'd also seen some blow away once, on the news. Mind you, The Boathouse didn't really look any more secure than the mobile homes, and I'd wanted to stay in that. Perhaps the fact that it was once a boat made it seem a better bet in wet and windy weather. Although I know that is completely irrational.

Anyway, I was very glad I was staying at the Sunrise B&B. And Lilith Shoe seemed nicer than I'd expected.

Three

Lilith returned from the funeral and tapped on my door. I'd fallen asleep in the chair so I'm not sure how long she was tapping and I was surprised to see that it was now dark outside. And that it was still snowing. A quick peek through the window pane revealed a layer of at least an inch or so on the sill. When I opened the door, Lilith beamed at me and handed me a glass filled with something resembling custard. It had a chocolate flake and a heavenly-smelling cinnamon stick leaning against the side and two dark red cherries floated on a teensy island of chocolate-dusted cream.

'I thought you might like to try my homemade egg-nog.'

'Oh. Er. Thank you. It looks ... delicious.'

I took the proffered glass, and the abundance of brandy made my eyes smart.

'It'll put hairs on your chest.'

She grinned as if that was something I

might want, although I knew it was merely an expression. What I was more concerned about was the brandy stripping the insides of my throat but I took a tiny sip and I was pleasantly surprised. Not only was it delicious, it was smooth and creamy and slid down a treat. I wouldn't have minded a larger glass of the stuff.

'Would you like to come in?'

I stepped to one side so that she could enter but she stayed exactly where she was.

'Thank you, dear, but no. I must get on.'

I smiled and nodded. 'Of course. Thank you for the egg-nog. Oh. How was the funeral?'

She glanced from left to right as if she suspected eavesdroppers and when she spoke, her voice was low.

'Well I'm not one to gossip but...' she leaned closer, her ample bosom almost pressed against my arm. 'Bernice Dunn won't be missed by anyone, save for her son – the gorgeous and talented Alex. He's a heart surgeon, you know, and the best in the business, or so Bernice would have had us all believe. Bit of a mother's boy though. Tied to her apron strings, he was. But that didn't stop him from chasing every woman he laid eyes on. That poor wife of his. Mind you, dear Diana's making up for that now. What's good for the goose is also sauce for the gander.' She shook her head and tutted.

'Bernice Dunn? That's whose funeral it was?'

'Yes, dear. And I know I shouldn't speak ill of the dead, but it's not a day too soon, some people might say. Although Alex will be lost without her. Especially now Diana's divorcing him. Between you and me, Diana's been seeing Mikkel Meloy, the owner of The Seahorse Inn amongst other properties. And when I say seeing, I mean that in the liberal sense of the word. They're doing a darn sight more than *seeing* one another. But she stood beside her husband today. The poor man looked utterly crushed. I don't believe he said more than two words to anyone. Oh. I saw Elsie, but I didn't tell her you were here. Although I did give her a smile and tell her that she might be in for a lovely, big surprise. Elsie never liked Bernice either, so she wasn't in the least bit upset. So, my dear, have you settled in and found everything you need?'

I was still trying to take in the fact that the body in the coffin had been that of Bernice Dunn. I'd never met her and had no reason to mourn her, but after Lilith had mentioned the Dunns to me earlier, I'd pondered as to why I knew that name. I'd eventually remembered it was because Alex Dunn was the husband of Diana, who was Aunt Elsie's sister's daughter. Basically, Aunt Elsie's niece. I'd never met Aunt Elsie's sister, Tabitha, or her children, but

Mum had mentioned them once or twice. I knew Diana had a twin called Josephine, but I knew nothing else about that family.

But if Bernice was Alex's mother, that meant she had been Diana's mother-in-law. Perhaps I should have attended the funeral after all. Just out of respect.

Should you attend the funeral of someone you don't know and haven't met, simply because they were the mother-in-law of someone who was related to your aunt – but not to you?

I had no idea. Mum would've known what to do.

She told me once that Diana and Josephine were what was known as my cousins-in-law, but that people often referred to such a relation, as a distant cousin.

As I never met them, I didn't give it much thought.

The odd thing was, we weren't close to our relatives, which was strange because Mum and Dad were the most wonderful, loving parents and they always said such lovely things about Aunt Elsie. Elsie didn't have any children and as far as I knew, she never married again after Uncle Eric died.

But I wondered why Aunt Elsie hadn't told me about Bernice in her note. Or in the content of the round robin letter. Surely that was worth mentioning?

Perhaps she didn't want to put a dampener on people's Christmases by mentioning a death.

'Yes thanks,' I said, seeing Lilith giving me a questioning look. 'We've settled in perfectly. The room is gorgeous and so is the view. And it's so cosy. Are there many other guests here at the moment? I didn't hear anyone moving about while you were gone.'

Lilith shook her head. 'Only you at the moment, dear. But more guests arrive tomorrow, and I'm fully booked over Christmas and the New Year. Just the way I like it. It's still snowing and the roads might get a bit icy. I don't usually provide evening meals, but as it's your first night here and the weather's bad, I'll be more than happy to make you something tonight. In fact, I could use the company. Funerals always make me sad. Unless you've already made plans, that is.'

I hadn't.

'Nope. No plans at all. I was just going to take Merry for a walk into the village and get something to eat and after that, have a relaxing bath and an early night. But I don't want to put you to any trouble.'

Her green eyes lit up like emeralds. 'No trouble, dear. I'll make one of my famous steak and mushroom pies, and your lovely friend here can have some of the offcuts.' She nodded her head in Merry's direction and didn't seem at all concerned that Merry was sprawled across the bed. 'Unless you're a vegetarian?'

'No. Steak and mushroom pie sounds fantastic. I'm happy to lend a hand if you like.'

'Oh no, dear. You're a guest. You just sit and relax. We'll eat at 6.30, if that's all right with you because if I eat later than that, I'll be up all night with indigestion.'

'That's perfect. I'll take Merry for a walk to stretch our legs, and we'll go for another after dinner. I assume it's safe to walk around here at night?'

'Absolutely. Nothing bad ever happens in Seahorse Harbour. Oh, wait. That's not strictly true. We had a spate of burglaries this summer, but the crooks were soon apprehended, so don't you worry. You might want to take a torch with you though. The street lights are few and far between. And stay away from the cliff-edge at night. It can be deceptive and you might think you're on a safe path only to realise you're not. In this weather, you wouldn't be able to see it anyway.'

'Don't worry. Merry is a bit boisterous so we'll be staying away from the cliff-edge while we're here.'

'I'll leave you to it then and I'll call you when dinner's ready.'

I closed the door behind her and finished the drink she'd given me. It was definitely very potent and the chocolate and the cherries were exceedingly moreish. I hoped Lilith might offer me more of her egg-nog during my stay.

'Come along then, Merry. Let's venture out into the snow and go for a little walk into the village.'

Merry's head shot up and her tail thwacked the bedspread. That dog could be sound asleep but the minute anyone said the word 'walk' it was as if she had supersonic hearing. She gave a small but enthusiastic bark and jumped off the bed.

It was quite a different story when I opened the front door a few minutes later. Merry had been pulling at her lead until then but once the door was opened and she saw the layer of white, and more snowflakes adding to it, she stopped in her tracks and looked up at me as if to say she'd changed her mind and didn't want to go out, after all.

'The fresh air will do us both some good.'

I'm not sure if I was trying to convince her or me. The air was bitterly cold now and the snow flurries swirled in front of us like tiny tornadoes. Sunrise B&B was so warm and cosy that the thought of venturing out definitely wasn't that appealing.

A moment later, Merry raced outside, tugging me along with her. She might be small but she's as strong as an ox. She'd obviously spotted something but I had no idea what. I couldn't see anything moving on the other side of the dimly lit road, apart from the hedge, but as we got closer, I spotted a robin flying out of Merry's way.

'You should be tucked up somewhere warm,' I said, as if the robin could hear me.

Mum loved robins. She always said that if you saw a robin it was a good omen and that they brought messages from loved ones who were no longer with us. Quite how they did that, she failed to explain.

'Sometimes you simply need to have faith,' she said.

I was so preoccupied wondering if this particular robin had brought a message from Mum and Dad that I only just remembered in time that on the other side of the hedge was yet another cliff. This one was only about a drop of fifteen feet or so into the gardens of the houses in The Heights, the road below Rock Road, but even so. Fifteen feet was a long way to fall, especially for a spaniel. I tugged Merry's lead and made sure I kept her close to me. Thankfully, now that the robin had departed, she'd lost interest and we walked calmly ahead, the only sounds being the lapping sea against the cliffs, and the scrunch of snow beneath my boots.

We turned right onto Seahorse Cliffs road and walked down towards the village. There was a large open space of what I'm sure was grass beneath the blanket of snow and Merry and I made fresh tracks in the pristine layer. I could see the gardens and hedges of the cottages in Meadow Lane and could hear some children laughing gleefully in the distance. They were probably making snow-people or having snowball fights, even though it was dark, but it was only a little after 5 so they were no doubt having fun before being called indoors for their tea.

One or two of the gardens had those awful, dazzling spotlights that lit up the space as bright as day. I know they were supposed to deter intruders but did they have to be quite so glaring?

The rest of the gardens had colourful or plain white fairy lights decorating the hedges and the rear of the cottages. Some even had a snowman, or Santa, or reindeers on the roofs. The inflatable kind, of course. Not the real ones.

Other than hearing the children, Merry and I didn't see another living soul as we wandered towards Church Row, with its cottages and houses giving off a very festive glow. Each cottage had a cheerful-looking wreath on the door and lights strung across the façade.

The shops were extremely Christmassy, the windows filled with wonderful items and one in particular really caught my attention. It was a seasonal display of felt mice having a jolly time in what was supposed to be a person's living room. There were tiny ropes of colourful ribbon hanging from a coffee table covered with beautifully wrapped gifts. Some of the mice – who were all dressed in red, green, or other holiday colours, climbed either up or down the ribbons while others looked as if they were peeking into the gifts. Some sat on a plate of faux mince pies, one with its belly so rounded it looked fit to burst. A couple of the mice were curled up on the armchair, and another read a book at least five times its own size and propped up against a red and gold cushion. A faux fire burned to one side of the display and the whole thing was so cosy that I wanted to step into the window and curl up with those gorgeously cute mice. But Merry would probably try to play with them.

Merry's sudden bark made me jump and a moment later, a tall, dark figure appeared from nowhere and raced towards me. For a split second, I foolishly thought I was about to be mugged, but the voice that greeted me sounded friendly – and rather deep and sexy, and made me breathe a sigh of relief.

'Hello, gorgeous! Lovely weather, isn't it?'

My heart did a rather surprising flutter and my cheeks burned as I looked at a set of long dark lashes on an exceedingly handsome face with a clean-shaven jaw. The man was at least seven or eight inches taller than me, so over six foot, solidly built and looked like the outdoorsy-type, with hair a sort of treacly colour and skin showing evidence of what was left of a tan. He was dressed in a tracksuit and a weatherproof jacket and was clearly just out running. His heavenly smile made me forget where I was for a second or two – until I realised that he hadn't been speaking to me. His compliment was clearly directed at Merry as he bent down and stroked her, tickling her under her chin. Her tail wagged to and fro and she panted with excitement. I couldn't blame her. I'd have done the same if this sexy hunk of a man had done that to me.

'Are you here on holiday?' he finally asked. 'Or did you come for the funeral?'

He was still looking at Merry so I didn't answer at first but he eventually glanced up at me with another smile and a questioning look in his startlingly bright eyes.

'Oh, er. Holiday. Well, visit, really. I've come to see my aunt.'

He stood up and met my gaze and I felt myself blush even more.

'Your aunt? That's nice. I don't think we've met. I'm Asher. Asher Bryant.'

He held out his hand and I took it. Even through my gloves I felt a warmth that sent a tingle or two racing up my spine.

'Hi. I'm Lottie Short. And this is Merry.'

'Lottie? That's short for Charlotte I

assume?'

'Yes. Asher's an unusual name.'

He looked thoughtful for a second or two.

'Not as unusual as my sister's. Her name's Sorcha. Are you staying for the holidays?'

'I think so. I'm not really sure. The room is booked until the day after Boxing Day but we'll see how things go.'

'Oh? Don't you get on with your aunt?'

'I hardly know her. I've only met her a few times in my life. She seems lovely and my parents were always singing her praises, so I'm sure it'll be fine.'

A frown furrowed his brows. 'You said, "were". Does that mean your parents have passed away? Sorry. That's none of my business.'

'Don't worry. It's fine. But yes. They both passed away three years ago, within a month of one another.'

'I'm so sorry. That must have been a terrible time for you.'

'It was. What about you?' I wanted to change the subject before I became too emotional. Even after three years, it sometimes felt as if I'd lost them only yesterday. 'Do you live here, or are you visiting?'

'I live here. In fact, if you look directly ahead, past the pub, you can just see the edge of my cottage. It's the pink one on the end of Rope Way. Pop in and say hi if you're passing.

And if this gorgeous little lady here ever needs a vet during your stay, I'm your man. I hope she doesn't, of course.'

'You're a vet? Gosh. That's good to know. Merry is sometimes a little accident-prone, so it's a relief to discover I won't have far to go if anything untoward should happen.'

He held my gaze for a moment or two and then began jogging on the spot.

'I suppose I'd better get back to my run. It was lovely to meet you both. I hope I'll see you again soon. Enjoy your stay in Seahorse Harbour.'

'Thanks. It was lovely to meet you too.'

I would never wish any harm at all on Merry but as I watched Asher Bryant run off up the hill towards Seahorse Cliffs, seemingly unhindered by the depth of snow, I sincerely hoped I'd see him again.

Four

Obviously, I asked Lilith about Asher Bryant when we sat down to dinner and the woman was a font of information. I already knew he was a vet, where he lived, and that he had a sister called Sorcha, but Lilith told me everything else I needed to know. And quite a lot I didn't.

'Asher and his family came here for a holiday years ago, and Asher fell in love with the place. Everyone does, of course, but this village seems to draw certain people to it. I think it has a magical quality. My dearly departed husband, God rest his soul, always said it was the seahorses, you know. That they send out vibrations into the world and bring people who will help them, or the village, in some way. Some people say that's nonsense, but it isn't. It's the God's honest truth.'

'I must admit I think there's something magical about seahorses,' I agreed.

I wasn't sure about them sending out

vibrations but I kept my scepticism to myself.

'There absolutely is, my dear.' Lilith leant forward and tapped my hand, knocking my food off my fork and back onto my plate. 'Perhaps they've called to you? Perhaps that's why you're here?'

'It would be lovely to think so, but I'm just here to see my aunt. And because ... well, I needed a little break.' I wasn't going to tell her all about Clark, or that I'd lost my job and had come here because I didn't have anywhere else to go and didn't want to be alone. I didn't want her sympathy or pity. 'You were telling me about Asher.'

'Oh yes. Where was I? Asher and his family. I can't recall exactly when they came to stay, but I think it was the last two weeks of August in the summer of 1998 and Asher was sixteen at the time. He's thirty-eight now.'

That seemed pretty exact to me. Lilith must have an exceedingly good memory.

'Asher found an injured seagull with a broken wing and took it to the vet, Barney Short. Oh goodness me. Your surname's Short! You're not related to Barney, are you?'

'Er, no. Not as far as I'm aware. It's just a strange coincidence.'

'Hmm. Or Fate. Barney Short was so good. Not that Asher isn't. Asher's a remarkable vet. That's why the seahorses wanted him. Asher and Barney hit it off the moment Asher walked in the door. He spent the rest of his holiday helping out around the place and decided there and then that he would be a vet. We were all so pleased when he came here and eventually took over the practice from Barney. And Asher's a Seahorse Rider, you know. They're all volunteers and they help look after the seahorses. They monitor the seagrass and the water. They keep the beaches clean and organise others to do likewise. They deter would-be seahorse hunters who might try to take the seahorses for pets or souvenirs, and they raise awareness of the plight of the darling little creatures, along with much-needed funds to help save them. There's a small sea life centre on Sea Walk where children from nearby schools come to learn about the seahorses and other marine life and it's where The Seahorse Riders' offices are based. That's where Asher can be found when he's not in his surgery, or on the water, or running around the village keeping fit. But he's sometimes in the pub. He's not all work, work, work. That young man also knows how to play, if you catch my drift.'

She winked at me and tapped my hand again but this time I managed to prevent the piece of her delicious steak and mushroom pie from falling off my fork.

'The Seahorse Riders sound incredible. It always astonishes me that some people are so dedicated to a certain cause. I don't think I've ever felt that strongly about anything.'

'Me neither, dear. Apart from my dearly departed husband. I felt very strongly about him. Not always in a good way.' She grinned and winked again.

'Does Asher have a girlfriend?'

I tried to make it sound as if it were merely curiosity and not because I'd quite like to be considered for the role. Ever since I'd seen Asher Bryant, I couldn't get his face out of my mind's eye. I'd thought about him all the way up the hill. I thought about him when I got changed. I thought about him when I glanced out of the window of my room and tried to see if his cottage was visible from there. It wasn't, sadly. And the moment we sat down to dinner I asked about him. For the first time in the last two years I'd thought about a man other than Clark.

Lilith's grin broadened.

'Got a little crush on Asher, have we? I don't blame you one bit. He's gorgeous. And no. He doesn't have a girlfriend.' She leant forward again. 'Now I'm not one to gossip but between you and me, he did have a bit of a thing for Josie Parnell this summer. They even dated a couple of times. He fell for her, I'm sad to say. But Josie already had her heart set on Liam. Liam Fulbright, that is. He's a ceramicist and he owns Fulbright Ceramics. That's in The Olde

Forge, opposite the church. Josie was over here from New York to stay with her sister, Diana, and Liam isn't the type of man to have a summer fling. He has a daughter, you know. Orla's sixteen and Liam adores her. It looked as if Liam wasn't interested in Josie, but he was. Anyone could see he was in love with her. But he'd been badly hurt by his wife, Una and before Una died, she told him she'd been unfaithful. You'll never guess who with. Alex Dunn. The man whose mother was cremated today and the husband of Josie's sister. Oh, the stories I could tell you about this village and the goings on. But as I said, I'm not one to gossip.'

'No. Of course. So Asher and Josie only dated a couple of times? What happened with Josie and Liam? Did she go back to New York?'

'Good heavens, no. Didn't I say? Once Josie told Liam that she loved him, Liam admitted he felt the same. The silly man couldn't bring himself to tell her until he'd heard the words from her. I think he hadn't really admitted it to himself until then. Men are odd creatures. But he'd only gone and bought himself and Orla tickets to go and visit Josie in New York! And on the day she was due to leave, too. I heard that from Orla so I know it's true. They changed the dates, as Josie had decided she wasn't going back, and they all went there last week. They went to see Josie's friends, do some Christmas shopping and go ice skating at the ice rink you always see on TV. The one at the Rockefeller Center. They had a wonderful time, so Orla tells me. And I'm sure they did.'

'Is Asher over Josie now, do you think?'

'I'm sure he is. He and Liam are close friends. Asher wants Liam to be happy and if that means curing himself of any feelings he had for Josie, that's exactly what he'd do.'

'I hope I see him again while I'm here. Does he usually spend Christmas in the village, do you know, or does he spend it with his family? I assume they don't live around here?'

'I heard him say, just the other day, that his family will be coming to visit him at some point over Christmas. His sister Sorcha was married, you know, but her husband treated her very badly and, with Asher's help, she eventually left him. She's four years younger than Asher and she's now back home with the parents, but she comes here every so often to stay with Asher. I thought she might move here permanently, but the seahorses haven't called to her. Yet. Perhaps they will when they think she's ready. Or perhaps they don't want her around. They're sensitive souls.'

Quite how she knew seahorses were sensitive souls was beyond me, but I didn't see any point in challenging this assumption. And they do look sensitive. There's something ethereal about them. Not that I'd ever seen one in the flesh. I'd only seen them on TV and on the website for Seahorse Harbour.

But that was something I could change. I'd read a bit about the sea life centre and it wasn't only kids who could go there to learn about the seahorses; adults could go too. That was one place I was definitely going to visit during my stay. And not just because I might see Asher Bryant there.

'Perhaps I'll get to meet her if she comes to stay this Christmas.'

'Perhaps. Now tell me all about the relationship between you and Elsie. If she is your aunt, surely you must know Diana and Josie? And possibly, Alex and Bernice?'

I explained that my relationship to Elsie was by marriage, not by blood, and that not only had I hardly got to know Elsie, I'd never met the separate branches of Elsie's family.

'Mum and Dad kept in contact with Elsie after her husband, my uncle Eric, died. He was my mum's younger brother. But Elsie never came to stay, at least not after my uncle's death, and we never visited her. Mum did mention Elsie's sister and the children, once or twice, so I have heard Diana and Josephine's names, but I've never met them. Our only connection to Elsie was my uncle and it seemed that after he'd gone, Elsie's life went in a different direction. But Mum and Dad always thought highly of her and when she came to Dad's funeral, she invited me to come and visit. It's just taken me a few years to do so.'

'Well I never. Elsie is so close to her nieces, Diana and Josie, and to her great-niece and great-nephew too. That's Diana's children, Becca and Toby. How odd that she chose not to maintain a close relationship with her husband's side of the family? But I do know that Elsie has a dislike of commitment and she's a free spirit when it comes to relationships. I also know she travelled extensively before she eventually bought Seaside Cottage and settled here. Josie is her favourite, you know. I think that's because Josie takes after her. Now I'm not one to gossip, as you know, but Josie was a bit of a wild child before she fell in love with Liam this summer. That girl has had more than her fair share of men, I'm pretty certain of that. And so has Elsie. Why only this summer she was dating Gray Meloy. He's Mikkel's dad, and he's now gone back to Norway or wherever it was he came from, but between you and me, I think he was hoping Elsie would invite him to stay.'

'Really? I look forward to my aunt telling me all about that. This dinner was delicious, Lilith. Thank you so much. But if you don't mind, I think I should take Merry for her final walk before bed and then have that bath I mentioned, and an early night. The journey seems to have taken it out of both of us. But I'll do the washing up before I go.'

She seemed a little surprised by my abrupt halt to the conversation and I suppose it might have been a little rude of me, but I felt uncomfortable discussing my aunt's love life with a total stranger. Although that hadn't stopped me listening to every word she had to say about Asher Bryant, or my distant cousin, Josie.

'Oh. I'm glad you enjoyed it, dear. But don't you worry about the washing up. I'll just pop it all in the dishwasher before I retire for the night. You and dear little Merry run along and enjoy yourselves. If there's anything you need, you know where I am. Breakfast is between 8 and 9, but as it's only you and Merry for now, I'm happy to change that just for tomorrow.'

'Thanks. But 8 is fine. I'll probably be up and about long before then to take Merry out for her morning pee. I'll say goodnight then, if you're sure there's nothing I can do to help.'

'Nothing at all. Good night, my dear and pleasant dreams. I don't need to be a genius to guess who you'll be dreaming about. Asher Bryant, I don't doubt.'

She grinned broadly and winked at me as Merry got up from the cushion Lilith had kindly placed in a cosy corner for her, and together we walked towards the hall.

I stopped at the door and turned to Lilith, smiling as warmly as I could.

'Please don't mention to anyone that I quite liked Asher Bryant. I'd be embarrassed if he found out. Especially as I only chatted to him for about 5 minutes.'

She beamed at me and tapped the turned-up tip of her nose.

'Your secret is safe with me, dear. As you know, I'm not one to gossip.'

Five

Waking up in a strange bed is always a little disorientating, however comfortable it may be. Waking up to the sound of waves crashing against cliffs not too far away and then seeing snow-laden clouds and at least three inches of pristine snow on the ground, was so much more than that.

It took me a few seconds to remember where I was. And that had nothing to do with drink. Although I will admit that when I returned with Merry from our pre-bedtime walk, I discovered Lilith had placed a tray with a large glass of her egg-nog outside my room, and as I was cold and the delicious, alcohol-laced beverage was there, I did knock it back before I went to sleep.

I think I was starting to see why Lilith's guests returned year after year and why her rooms were usually booked months in advance. Lilith Shoe had a knack of making her guests feel welcome.

I'd been lucky to get this room, especially as it had been due to a last-minute cancellation. A party of people had booked out the entire B&B and then, due to unforeseen circumstances, or so they had apparently said, they'd cancelled the booking the very morning I was looking for a place to stay. Most of the rooms had gone to others on a waiting list and this was the only room she had left.

'It was clearly meant to be,' Lilith had said when I'd seen the sudden vacancy on- line and had immediately called her up to book it.

I'd been looking for over an hour and had almost decided I'd have to stay in the nearby town of Easterhill, a few miles inland to the north of Seahorse Harbour. Assuming there were vacancies somewhere there. Or I'd have to opt for one of the mobile homes in the Holiday Park as The Boathouse was full and so was the Sunrise B&B. That was about it when it came to holiday accommodation in this village. But for some reason, I'd clicked back to take another look at the Sunrise B&B even though it was full, and the vacancy had popped up.

Perhaps, Lilith was right. Perhaps it was meant to be.

I glanced at my watch and couldn't believe the time. It was almost 7.15 and I never slept past 6 normally. It must have been the sea air.

Even Merry, who was usually licking my face if my eyes weren't open by 5 past 6, yawned, shook her head and threw me a look as if to say, 'Let's have another half an hour.'

When she finally realised I had showered and dressed and that we'd be going out, she dragged herself off the bed and trotted to the window. I burst out laughing when I saw the expression in her eyes after she had peered outside. Her head shot round, her jaw dropped open and her eyes seemed to bulge from beneath her eyelids. If she'd been human, she would've used a few expletives, I'm sure, and told me in no uncertain terms that I must be having a laugh if I expected her to go out in that.

'I'm sure it's not as bad as it looks,' I said.

She hung her head and didn't seem convinced.

I spotted someone walking briskly across the road towards the B&B and recognised Lilith, from the shape and size of her and her bright ginger hair sticking out at all angles beneath a knitted green bobble hat. Where on earth had she been at this time in the morning? She appeared to be carrying a couple of loaves of bread. Two long French sticks were evident in her shopping bag. Had she been out to get bread for my breakfast? That made me feel a pang of guilt. But why French sticks? That wasn't your normal 'breakfast bread'.

'Come on, Merry. Let's go and find out.'

I picked up the lead and Merry's coat and

shrugged on my own, together with a hat, hopping into my boots as I walked. We met Lilith in the hall.

'Good morning, Lilith. How are you today? I hope you haven't been out because of us.'

'Morning! Did you sleep well? I hope I didn't wake you when I left. And no. I always go out first thing and buy freshly baked bread from Bev at Beach Bakers. Bev makes the best bread for miles around and I do love a French stick, don't you? I've bought a wholemeal loaf too, in case you might prefer that. It's bitter out there this morning but I see you're wrapped up warm.'

'I love any bread, especially with lashings of butter and marmalade. We won't be out for long. Just for Merry to have a pee and stretch her legs. We'll only be about fifteen minutes, if that's okay?'

'Yes, yes, yes. Take as long as you like. I'll make breakfast as soon as you come back. Oh. But you'll never guess who I saw out running this morning.'

I could tell from the expression on her face. It was half excitement, half guilt. She'd seen Asher Bryant and unless I was very much mistaken, she had mentioned me.

'Asher?'

She nodded joyfully. 'The very same. I told him he needs his head examined going out running in this weather. He said he was warm and he enjoyed the bracing air. Well, I told him there were far better ways to keep warm and what he should be doing was embracing a young lady, and that I might know one who could help with that. Now don't give me that look, dear. It was just a little joke and I didn't mention you by name. I just said I had a very pretty guest staying with me at the moment, who I happened to know was single.'

'You didn't?'

'Oh yes, I did. And he smiled and said he thought he'd already met you. And you'll never guess what else he said, so I'll tell you. He said, "Pretty, doesn't do her justice, Lilith". What do you think of that? I think things might be warming up very nicely with you and Asher.'

I didn't know whether to laugh, cry or throw a tantrum, but the truth was, I felt a rather warm glow when she repeated Asher's words. Did he honestly think I was more than pretty?

Mind you, it had been dark when we'd met, so perhaps he hadn't really got a good look at me. Or perhaps he was talking about Merry. After all, she was the one he'd called 'gorgeous' yesterday, not me.

But how did Lilith know I was single? I don't recall telling her. In fact, I'm pretty sure I'd been careful not to mention my relationship status at all. I suppose, as I was going to be spending Christmas in a B&B with just my dog

59

that was a natural assumption for her to make.

Six

After breakfast, which consisted of fresh grapefruit, a full English, fresh bread plus wholemeal toast together with lashings of butter and marmalade, plus enough coffee to sink a battleship, Merry and I ventured outside once more. We'd only been out for about five minutes earlier. It had been far too cold to stay out for longer than that. But an hour or so later, full to bursting, I decided we needed to get some bracing fresh air and walk off some of that delicious breakfast.

We walked as briskly as we could but our progress was hampered by the depth of the snow. At least the earlier icy wind that had whipped up my hair and tugged at Merry's long ears, had dropped and the temperature felt a few degrees warmer because of that. It was now around 9 but we seemed to be the only ones foolish enough to be outside.

Other than the waves which were no longer crashing against the cliffs now that the tide was going out but were still swishing and swooshing angrily at the sand, and a few squawking gulls arguing over their breakfast of scraps from the bins or discarded food, the place was silent. Not one car passed us as we made our way down the road from Seahorse Cliffs towards the village centre. I did notice other footprints, so people had been about. Perhaps they were Lilith's. Or maybe Asher's.

I shouldn't have thought about Asher. That reminded me of what Lilith had said and even now my face burned with embarrassment. I hope he didn't think I'd been discussing him with Lilith.

Even though I had.

I stopped again at the shop window with the felt mice, and smiled at the display. I spotted someone moving around inside the shop and realised it was open.

Of course it was. It was gone 9 on a Saturday morning so even in a village, the shops would be open by now. Especially as this was the last Saturday before Christmas.

I was tempted to go in and look around but I couldn't see anywhere to tie Merry's lead so I'd have to do my browsing another time. That was the one issue with being a dog-owner. Unless shops provided a rail, a hook, or something to which a lead could be tied, we couldn't leave our beloved pets outside and go in to browse.

There wasn't even a drainpipe, or a lamppost nearby. Not that I'd ever leave Merry tied to something near the road. As I mentioned, she likes to chase things. She's not the sort of dog to sit patiently, her gaze fixed firmly on the entrance, waiting for her owner to reappear. And definitely not if something catches her eye.

We proceeded past the other two shops and the car park of the pub when the sudden and extremely loud peel of bells almost gave me a heart attack. Even Merry jumped around to see where the noise was coming from. For such a small church, those bells were deafening, but we were standing directly opposite the bell tower. After the initial shock, they sounded melodious.

I couldn't see the lychgate from where I stood as the entrance to the church was hidden by the trunk of the ancient oak but I heard a cheery voice call out, 'Good morning.'

I wasn't sure if the person was greeting me, or someone else as I scanned for a glimpse of the speaker, but I decided to err on the side of caution and replied with an equally cheery, 'Good morning.'

Nothing further was said, so Merry and I continued on our way, but I did glance over my shoulder once or twice in the hope of seeing someone. I suddenly had an irrational thought that the greeting might have come from a ghost in that graveyard. But of course that was fanciful nonsense. Although I couldn't see a living soul.

I'd been tempted to walk towards Church Hill and then past Asher's cottage on Rope Way. I could see the cottage from where we were but instead, I took the turning before, called Sand Lane and walked past The Seahorse Inn. After what Lilith had said to Asher, I thought it might look as if I were stalking him or something if he glanced out of his window and saw me go past.

The Seahorse Inn looked exactly as it had on the website, which I suppose it should have done. It was painted cerise pink and had a thatched roof and a blackened oak front door and looked as ancient as the oak tree outside the church opposite. The sign hanging to one side of the pub door was of a seahorse and the name was written in the oval, cast iron surround. It creaked a little as it began to swing gently to and fro in the slight breeze that had picked up again.

I peered in the window as I passed and the inside appeared to be far more modern and rather eclectic. I could see a log fire burning in a hearth at one end of the pub. If dogs were allowed inside, I'd definitely pop in for a glass of wine later. Or maybe a Bailey's. It was the festive season, after all.

I felt a warm glow just thinking about

sitting beside that fire. Imagine how much cosier it would be to sit beside that fire with someone special.

Once again, a vision of Asher Bryant popped into my head. Still, that was so much better than a vision of Clark Corne, who I bet was sitting in front of a roaring fire every day and every night in the ski chalet he and his friends had rented. But I dismissed all thoughts of him from my mind. I could survive without Clark. Not that I really had a choice.

The door to the pub was closed but I read a sign on it that informed me the premises opened at 11 a.m. every day and that food was served from noon until 2 and again from 6 until 10 in the evening. Last orders for drinks was 11, so presumably it closed shortly after that.

The door also displayed a colourful flyer, again with a seahorse in the background, giving details of the Hippocampus Restaurant on Sea Walk, and a dark blue and silver flyer advertising Neptune's Nightclub. I suppose that was because Mikkel Meloy owned all three places.

I'd definitely visit the pub and the restaurant while I was here, but I wouldn't be going to a nightclub on my own. I didn't think Aunt Elsie would be interested in going with me to a place like that.

Assuming she and I got on, that is. She might not even invite me in, especially if she didn't like dogs. I hadn't really thought this through but I knew that I was on my way to Aunt Elsie's cottage. I was intending to wait a day or two and get my bearings in the village before I went to see her, but as soon as I saw the sign for Church Hill as I stood opposite the church, I knew that I would be going to see my aunt today.

Church Hill was the longest road in the village, according to the map I'd looked at earlier on my phone, thanks to Google. It led from the top of a very steep hill to the north of the church, down past Wood Lane and Rope Way and skirted the length of Sea Walk, right the way to the entrance to Seahorse Harbour Holiday Park.

Seaside Cottage, which was where Aunt Elsie lived was situated on a raised bank on the corner of Wood Lane and Church Hill, but the front entrance was actually the first home on Church Hill.

Walking down Sand Lane, with the pub on one side and the beautiful gardens opposite, called Memorial Gardens according to the plaque, I couldn't see Elsie's cottage, but again, I'd had a sneaky peek courtesy of various maps on the internet.

I'd even seen inside, thanks to a couple of property marketing websites. Although those photos had been from the time when the cottage was on the market, before Aunt Elsie bought it just a few years ago, and it might not be the same now as it was in those images. Elsie might've changed it. But then again, she might not.

I wouldn't mention I'd done that when I did meet her though. Some people might possibly see that as an invasion of their privacy.

It really was worrying what could be found on the internet these days. For example, I didn't know when Elsie had moved to Seahorse Harbour, but all I needed to do to find out was enter the address and look for 'sold properties in the area'. Details of all sales popped up in a helpful list giving the house numbers, the month and year the property was sold, and a link to any relevant sales details from the past. I even knew how much she paid for it.

At the end of Sand Lane was a large store, the sign of which read: The General Store. This was clearly the village supermarket, although a quick glance in the massive glass windows, covered in large, white, cut-out snowflakes and equally large, bright red stars declaring several bargains could be had, showed it sold virtually everything you might need – within reason. I could hear the Christmas music playing inside, from here and I could also see one or two people doing some shopping. I was a little relieved to see the village wasn't entirely deserted.

I stepped onto what I'd seen from my brief

research, was Sea Walk. Beneath the thick layer of snow were dark pink and dark purple paving slabs and the whole length of Sea Walk was pedestrianized.

I glanced along to my left and could see a couple of shops, plus Hippocampus Restaurant where a Christmas tree at least four metres high stood in a round, wooden tub. It was strung with bright white fairy lights and seahorse-shaped decorations, which I assumed must be weather-proof. They must also have been tied very tightly to the branches because Sea Walk was exposed to all the elements.

Beside that was Neptune's Nightclub with a deep bright blue and shiny façade. I had seen on the internet that each of the two large, glass doors had an image of the god himself etched into them, but I couldn't see the doors from where I stood.

I could see a sign to The Boathouse though, and most importantly, I could see Seahorse Tales, the sea life centre which had a bright turquoise façade and a teal roof, although the roof was currently covered by a blanket of snow.

Beyond that there were just snow-covered cliffs and I could see waves splashing against the cliffs of Seahorse Point where the headland protruded out into the sea.

I wondered if Asher was in his surgery or at the sea life centre right now. Not that it mattered. I needed to avoid him for today at least. Hopefully by tomorrow, he'd have forgotten what Lilith had said to him.

Turning to my right, with Merry keen to keep moving, I spotted Beach Bakers, where Lilith had come earlier for the bread. The window display was very festive with shelves containing mince pies, gingerbread biscuits, candy cane-shaped rolls, cinnamon swirls, several shapes and sizes of beautifully decorated Christmas cakes and so much more besides. Just looking at all those delights made my mouth water. The shelves were trimmed with rows of white bunting in the shapes of snowflakes, snowmen and reindeers and warm white lights glowed behind the pane of glass.

Before that though, and just next door, was a café called Seahorse Bites. Judging by the steamed-up windows, behind which a curtain of multi-coloured fairy lights twinkled, it was clearly busy, and even through the closed door I could smell bacon frying and fresh coffee brewing. If I hadn't been so full, I'd have wanted to go in, especially as a large sign and a picture of a scruffy-looking dog on the glass door stated, 'Dogs welcome, along with well-behaved humans.' That made me smile. The owner was clearly a dog-lover and someone with a sense of humour.

Nice Ice, the last building on Sea Walk, was closed for the winter, according to the sign on that. I don't suppose people wanted ice cream during this season, especially not on a day like today.

Opposite this row of shops was the wide sweep of sand, and the rocks which I'd seen from the internet formed the curly tail of the seahorse-shaped bay. The tide was still going out and the waves were topped with wild curls of white as they rushed over the sands. Some caught the edge of the rocks with resounding thuds, and threw spray high into the air. It was an awe-inspiring sight.

I turned my attention from the sea and spotted heavy clouds rolling down from the north. It looked as if we'd be having more snow. Possibly quite a lot. Not that I knew much about predicting the weather. But then neither did the experts. Last night's snow storm hadn't been forecast.

And then I saw Aunt Elsie's. I stopped for a moment and took a deep breath.

Seaside Cottage was just a short stroll up from Sea Walk and the cottage looked as if it had a direct view of Seahorse Point and the entire bay from the front. I knew from the various maps and images on the sales particulars that at the back was a tall hedge of holly, quince and forsythia. Behind that there was a wood called Little Wood, which led all the way up the hill behind several houses, which made the garden very secluded.

I'd seen photos of a sitting room, a kitchen diner and a pantry on the ground floor with two bedrooms and a bathroom on the next. There was also an attic and the sales details at the time Aunt Elsie purchased it four years ago had mentioned this could possibly be converted into a master bedroom with an en suite. I wondered if Elsie had done that. Well not her, obviously, but if she had had that done. The thatched roof certainly looked large enough, even to my untrained eye, but there wasn't a window in the roof at the front. Perhaps there was one at the rear, although I could see oeil-de-boeuf windows on each gable end wall, so perhaps they provided sufficient light.

As I got closer, I noticed a variety of winter flowers popping their heads above the snow. The front garden was small compared to the back garden, I recalled, and in the photos both had been somewhat overgrown. From the little I could see beneath the blanket of white, Aunt Elsie had definitely redesigned the front garden since she had bought the place.

Merry gave a nervous little bark as we approached the dark yellow front door of the sunshine yellow painted cottage. The festive wreath on the door was a massive ring of pine-scented spruce, gold glitter-covered pine cones, red-berried holly, creamy white-berried mistletoe, cinnamon sticks tied together with dark green twine, whole, dried citrus fruit, and red, gold and green ribbons entwined around it all.

At first I couldn't see the doorbell, but then I saw one of those video door bells to one side. Aunt Elsie apparently liked to see who was calling on her before she opened her door. And who could blame her for that? Especially if there had been burglaries just this summer, as Lilith had told me there had been.

'This is it, Merry.'

I smiled down at my companion who was shaking snow from the tips of the fur on her ears and her tummy and she glanced up at me and gave a supportive and encouraging bark.

You may not believe this, but I can tell the difference between the types of barks she makes. This one definitely said, 'You've got this. Now get me out of this snow and in front of a fire, please, Mum.'

I pressed the bell and waited and it was only a matter of seconds before the front door swung open and a somewhat surprised Aunt Elsie stood in the doorway, staring at me in disbelief.

I was quite surprised myself. The last time I'd seen her was at Dad's funeral, at which she wore a deep purple, long velvet dress and a purple and black velvet bolero- style jacket that had a vivid splash of lime green, like a bolt of lightning, across the front. I noticed it because it was so startling it was hard not to, and it matched the streak of lime green in her purple-dyed hair. Not strictly the sort of outfit you'd expect a woman in her sixties to wear.

Now, she was wearing a pair of bright red leggings emblazoned with images of mistletoe and holly and an emerald green, fluffy jumper that looked at least five sizes too big and stretched to just above her knees. It had a drunken-looking snowman with red flashing bulbs for eyes on the front and the words, 'Many Hicmas' scrawled haphazardly beneath him. And on her now red, green and white striped hair, she wore a headband with two springing reindeer antlers bouncing to and fro. Reindeer earrings that seemed to be flashing and dancing at the same time swung from her ears.

'Holy mopeds,' she said, looking me up and down and glancing briefly at Merry, shock etched clearly on her face, but her eyes bright with excitement. 'Is it really you, Lottie? Are you really here?' Concern replaced the excitement. 'Is everything all right?'

Seven

Seaside Cottage had changed considerably since Aunt Elsie had moved in four years ago and the ground floor looked nothing like it had in the sales details I'd seen.

Having reassured her that I was fine as she ushered me inside, and that I'd just decided it was time I paid her a visit, she seemed to relax a little. Now, as I followed her along the hall, past a coat stand, there was a kitchen directly ahead which I could see led out into the snow-covered garden. To our left were the stairs and to the right, a large sitting and dining room that ran from front to back.

'Let's sit in here,' Aunt Elsie said, standing aside so that I could enter first. 'There's a lovely log fire and Merry looks as if she might like to sprawl out in front of that.'

I was surprised that she remembered Merry's name and also that she was happy for my dog to sprawl out on what looked as if it might be an exceedingly expensive, antique silk, Persian rug, spread between two sumptuous-looking sofas and the hearth. I'd only seen Persian rugs in pictures, apart from once when I saw one that sold at an auction Dad took me to. It went for over £40,000. Even cheaper, genuine Persian rugs could sell for several thousand, and Dad told me that the most expensive one ever sold went for over 3 million dollars in New York.

As if reading my mind, Elsie laughed and said, 'The rug's an imitation. It may look like a genuine, antique silk, Persian rug, but a friend of mine in modern-day Persia, otherwise known as Iran, gave it to me as a birthday gift about ten years ago. I know he was pretty keen on me but he wouldn't have given me a rug worth thousands of pounds. I think he bought it from a local market stall.'

It was an impressive imitation; the colour fade and wear and tear were perfectly aged. But I didn't know much about such things, other than what I'd seen and read, so I'd take my aunt's word for it and as Merry had plonked herself down in the middle of it, it was too late to worry about it now.

Elsie beamed at me and shook her head as if she still couldn't believe I was there.

'Let me take your coat. Would you like a mug of hot chocolate? I was just about to make some.'

'Thanks. That would be lovely.'

I shrugged off my coat and handed it to her, together with my hat, scarf and gloves.

'Make yourself at home. I'll be back in a jiffy.'

She reached out a hand and gently squeezed my arm and an odd sensation swept over me. I had an overwhelming urge to hug her – and I had no idea where that feeling had come from. I didn't though and in a moment she was gone.

I caught my breath as I dropped onto the sofa facing the fire and strewn with Christmas cushions of all colours, shapes and sizes. Merry rolled over on the rug, and lay on her back, her paws bent in the air, her tongue flopping to one side and made a contented muffled bark before closing her eyes. She'd clearly made herself at home.

I perched on the edge of the sofa, my boots flat on the floor, knees tense, and hands twisting nervously in my lap. I could hear Aunt Elsie in the kitchen and Christmas carols playing in the background. What must she be thinking? Was she pleased to see me, or not? Did she have plans for today that my arrival had screwed up? I hadn't thought to ask.

The room was warm and cosy and other than the Christmas cushions on the matching, red sofas there were multi-coloured, Christmassy throws. In addition to the sofas was a glass coffee table, a large dark wood sideboard, and a tall and skinny, purple Christmas tree, every branch of which was hung with a coloured or sparkly bauble or small ornament, and piles of beautifully wrapped presents in a variety of festive paper tumbled beneath. It was garish and yet equally stunning.

At the other end of the long room was a glass dining table and eight sleek and modern, chrome and rainbow-coloured chairs. Near the folding, glass doors to the garden sat a small, real pine Christmas tree, on a table with a reindeer cloth on it. Rows of fairy lights were strung along the walls and around the windows and there were more lights in several hurricane glasses near the hearth.

'Here we are,' Elsie said, returning to the room a few minutes later and placing a tray with two mugs of hot chocolate topped with cream and covered in grated chocolate, on the glass coffee table. There was also a plate of delicious-looking mince pies, some running with icing, some not. 'Help yourself. They're still warm from the oven.'

She sat on the sofa opposite me, kicked off a pair of Christmassy mules, and curled her legs and feet beneath her, looking at me over the rim of her mug and the mountain of cream on top.

'Thanks.' I took an iced mince pie and one bite told me it was as scrumptious as it looked.

And that it contained more than a drop of brandy. I washed it down with a swig of hot chocolate which warmed my throat in more ways than one. 'Is there alcohol in the hot chocolate too?'

'Of course,' she said, as if I were crazy to ask. 'Festive hot chocolate has to be laced with either brandy or rum. We're having brandy today.'

'It's a good thing I won't be driving.' I smiled and took another swig. It really was divine hot chocolate. 'Er. I hope you don't mind my turning up on your doorstep. I'm staying at the Sunrise B&B in Rock Road for a few days. I was going to call but, well, I wasn't certain of my plans and it was a bit of a last-minute decision. And then I thought it might be a nice surprise. I hope I haven't upset any plans you might've had for today.'

'It's a *wonderful* surprise! And now I understand what Lilith meant at the funeral yesterday. You haven't upset any plans, so don't give that another thought. But why are you staying at the B&B? There's plenty of room for you here and you must know that I'd love to have you stay.'

'I didn't want to impose. And it's not just me, it's Merry too. I didn't know if you had a cat, or anything. And some people don't like dogs in their homes.'

She waved a hand in the air and several

rows of bangles jingled on her wrist.

'I have no pets. But I'm happy to have other people's come to stay. Merry is more than welcome. How long are you staying? A few days, I believe you said. Does that mean you'll be leaving before the Big Day or will you be here for that?'

'I've booked my room until the day after Boxing Day.'

'Excellent! We'll tell Lilith today that you're coming to stay with me.'

'No! I mean... I don't want to be any trouble. And I can't cancel the rest of my stay at the B&B. I only got the room due to a previous cancellation. I couldn't do that to Lilith. She's been so kind. And we've settled in, so it seems silly to move just for the sake of a few days. But ... I was hoping Merry and I could spend some time with you, if that's okay?'

She looked disappointed and even a little sad and I could see what Mum had meant when she'd said that my emotions were written on my face. I could see Elsie's in her eyes.

'Of course, it is. It's more than okay. But you wouldn't be any trouble if you moved in here. And Lilith will understand. Besides, I can pay her for the room so she won't be out of pocket.'

'No. I really couldn't ask you to do that.'

'You didn't ask. I offered.' She met my look and smiled tenderly. 'You don't have to decide right now. I can understand that you might want your privacy. We've only met a few times, haven't we? It's quite all right for you to be a bit wary. Let's see how today goes, shall we? And why don't we agree on this? I won't pester you to come and stay here, but I want you to know that nothing would make me happier. You're family, Lottie. And people should be with their family at Christmas.'

The doorbell, and Merry barking, cut our conversation short. Elsie put her mug on the coffee table and got up to answer the door. A little reluctantly, I thought. As if she cursed the intrusion from whoever was ringing her bell. But she sounded delighted when she opened the front door.

'Honey bee!' I heard her shout gleefully. 'You're just the person I need right now.'

Eight

Having never met Josephine Parnell I knew nothing much about her, but I seemed to recall being told that she and her twin sister, Diana were just over a year older than me, so when Elsie introduced the really pretty, woman she'd just brought into the room as Josie, the first thing I wondered was, would we become friends? She had her arm linked through Elsie's and a beaming smile on her face.

The second thing I wondered was why Josie's hair was chestnut brown on top with fiery red waves tumbling over her shoulders. Did everyone on Elsie's side of the family have their hair dyed in a variety of colours? Or was it just Elsie and Josie?

I noticed Josie had an hour-glass figure as she took off her coat and threw it on the back of one of the dining chairs, and she was just an inch or so shorter than me by the looks of it.

She also wore a Christmas jumper but hers wasn't as long as Elsie's; it just brushed the waistband of her jeans. It was bottle-green with a white Christmas tree decorated with softly flashing, multi-coloured lights.

Something else she and Elsie had in common. I felt drab in comparison with my jeans and plain navy-blue jumper. And my strawberry blonde hair was all one colour.

'This is your distant cousin, Josie,' Elsie said, smiling somewhat sheepishly at Josie and then at me. 'Josephine Parnell. I'm sure I've told you about her and Diana, and I know Lydia would've mentioned the Parnell twins.'

Josie was more stunned by this meeting than I was.

'My distant cousin? What cousin? How?'

'Oh.' Elsie shrugged. 'Didn't Tibby mention Lottie to you? Charlotte Short?'

'No. Mum never mentioned either a Lottie or a Charlotte Short. How are we cousins, exactly? And why the distant bit? Is Lottie from your husband's side of the family? And who is Lydia?'

She turned her attention to Elsie but she did give me a friendly smile.

'Yes. Yes she is. Lydia was my husband Eric's older sister.'

'And my mum,' I added. 'Hi, Josie. It's good to finally meet you. Mum did mention you and Diana and I don't know why we've never met. Tibby's your mum, isn't she? I wonder why she didn't tell you and your sister about me?'

'Well,' Elsie said, clearing her throat and beaming at both of us. 'All that matters is that you have met now. Take a seat honey bee and I'll get you some hot chocolate. I know I don't need to tell you to help yourself to a mince pie. But where are my manners? You haven't met Merry. And we all know how much you love dogs.'

Elsie laughed as she patted Josie's hand and pointed to Merry who clearly wasn't curious enough to get up from the rug and the warmth of the fire to go and investigate this new person. Come to that, Josie didn't seem that keen on going to introduce herself to my dog, either.

'You're a dog-lover?' I doubted that from the expression on her face.

Josie laughed and shook her head as Elsie walked away.

'Not exactly. I don't dislike them. It's just that my sister's dog, Henry and I have a bit of a love-hate relationship. Well, we did. Now I think he likes me and I've fallen for him in a big way, but I'm not good at looking after living things.'

'Liam and Orla will disagree with you on that,' Elsie called out from the kitchen. 'And Henry loves you now, as much as you love him.'

Josie smiled and her eyes lit up with love. She let out a wistful sigh.

'Liam's my boyfriend and Orla's his daughter.' She flopped onto the sofa opposite. 'He's a widower and he's wonderful. We've been together since the summer. Since August. Since my birthday, in fact. Although we sort of got together a bit before that. In a way.' Her smile broadened considerably, as if a special memory had popped into her head and then a second or so later she seemed to snap out of her dream-like state. 'So you and I are distant cousins? Wow! I honestly had no idea you existed until just now. Sorry. Do you live abroad? Are you here for Christmas? Are you staying with Elsie? She didn't tell us you were coming.'

I smiled at her. I liked her so far.

'I live in Reading, so not that far away. And although Mum and Dad did tell me you and Diana were my cousins-in-law they didn't mention you much. I got the impression that my mum and yours weren't at all close. I know they never even exchanged as much as a Christmas card. I asked once if there had been some sort of family rift but Mum said there hadn't. It was simply that the two families had never really spent any time together. Which is a bit odd seeing as Elsie was married to my mum's younger brother, whom Mum adored. Mum had definitely met your mum, but I think that, after my uncle Eric died, Elsie sort of drifted away from us. We're related by marriage, not by blood and I think that makes a difference.'

'I suppose it must have.' Josie looked thoughtful. 'It's odd though, isn't it? I mean, Mum did tell Diana and me about Uncle Eric but she never mentioned he had a sister or that his sister had a daughter. He died when we were about one or so, and Elsie hardly ever talks about him. Perhaps his death hit her harder than we knew and that's why she drifted away from you. Perhaps your mum was a reminder of what Elsie had lost?'

I got the distinct impression Josie was trying to convince herself of something as a way of understanding the situation. I'd never really questioned it myself until now. Was that why Elsie kept away from us?

I scanned the room but there wasn't one photo of Uncle Eric. Not one. Not even a wedding photo of his and Elsie's Big Day. My mum had loads of photos of Eric, including two from Elsie and Eric's wedding.

'Maybe,' I said.

And now I wanted to know. To understand why I'd hardly ever seen Elsie in spite of the fact that Mum and Dad adored her. And I must confess, I was a little surprised that Mum had told me about Diana and Josie but Elsie and Tabitha hadn't told them about me.

'Wait until I tell Diana,' Josie said, getting out her phone and texting, a huge grin on her face. 'She'll be down here faster than the speed of light.'

Elsie returned with Josie's hot chocolate. Josie smiled and took a large swig. Either Elsie hadn't laced hers with alcohol or Josie hadn't noticed.

'Are you getting to know one another?' Elsie said, resuming her seat on the sofa.

Josie leant towards her and I foolishly envied the close bond they clearly shared.

'Yep. And Diana should be here any minute because I've just texted her and told her there is someone here she has to meet. Oh.' She suddenly seemed flustered. 'But I wanted to tell you something.' She glanced at me and back at Elsie.

'Would you like some privacy?' I asked. 'I can go outside for a while, if you like.'

'Go outside?' Elsie repeated. 'That's not necessary, surely?'

Josie only needed a second before she smiled and shook her head.

'No. There's no need for that. You're family, even if it is just by marriage, so you're going to hear all about this soon anyway. But I'd better quickly fill you in before Diana gets here. Did you know Diana was married?'

'Yes. To Alex Dunn. A surgeon, I believe. But that's all I know other than they have two kids.'

'That's right. I'll have to tell you the long

and detailed story another time but here's the short version. We've known Alex since we were kids. Di and Alex married when they were still in their teens. He's a bit of a shit though and he's cheated on her for most of their married life, but she adored him. Until this summer. She finally came to her senses after falling for someone else. At least we all hoped she had. The guy who owns the local pub, as it happens. And a nightclub and restaurant. But that's not important. Alex idolised his mum, Bernice and she only had to tell him to do something and he did it. She died last week and Alex is devastated.' She glanced at Elsie.

'Yes,' I said. 'I arrived yesterday as the funeral was about to start. Lilith told me whose funeral it was and I must admit I was surprised. Especially because Aunt Elsie hadn't mentioned Bernice's passing, in her letter, or her note to me.'

'Oh,' Elsie said. 'Did you know who Bernice was? I never liked the woman so it didn't even occur to me to mention her. And it was all very sudden. I think I might've posted the cards on the very day it happened, in fact. So I couldn't have mentioned it even if I'd wanted to. It was a hit and run and Bernice was dead the minute the vehicle struck her. The police have no idea who the driver was.'

'That's awful,' I said. 'Especially at this time of year. Sorry. It's dreadful at any time of year, of course, but it does always seem worse to lose someone at Christmastime.'

I hung my head as memories of my last Christmas with Mum and Dad came flooding back. We knew Mum didn't have long but we'd tried to make that Christmas the best one we'd ever had. And then, just a few days later, she was gone.

Elsie's voice was soft and tender when she informed Josie that I'd lost my mum on New Year's Eve three years ago.

'I'm so, so sorry,' Josie said, and I could tell she was being sincere.

'Thank you.' I forced a smile. 'Sorry. You were telling us about Bernice and Alex and Diana.'

Elsie gave me a sympathetic smile and then a crease formed between her brows and she stared at Josie.

'Did you say, "we all hoped she had," when you said Diana had fallen for someone else? Are you telling me, sorry, us, that you have reason to doubt her feelings for Mikkel?'

Josie let out a loud sigh and nodded.

'It's because of Bernice. Naturally, Di had to invite Alex to stay at Sea View Cottage once she heard about the accident. And of course he had to stay on once he'd told Di that Bernice wanted her funeral to be held down here and not up in London. But the thing is, since he's been staying here, Diana has hardly seen

Mikkel. I know that for a fact because not only did Di tell me that but Mikkel did too. He actually asked me if I thought there was any chance that Di would take Alex back. I laughed and said, 'Not on your life', but now I'm not so sure.'

'What?' Elsie twisted in her seat to look Josie directly in the eye. 'Are you saying you think there may be?'

Josie nodded. 'That's what I came here to tell you today. I stayed on at the cottage, as you know, to help clear up after the funeral reception. Not that I needed to as Diana had hired help, but anyway. I really stayed on to make sure Diana and the kids were okay. Alex has been crying. A lot, apparently, according to Orla who has seen it for herself when she's been visiting Becca.' Josie glanced at me. 'Sorry. Liam's daughter, Orla, and Diana's daughter, Becca are best friends.'

'Ah. Thanks.'

'Anyway, Alex has been acting strangely too. Not just crying. Even Diana told me the other day that he seemed different, somehow. I didn't take much notice at the time. I thought he'd be bound to be suffering from shock. Grief changes people, we all know that. But I hadn't taken on board what was actually happening. Until last night when Di and I had a chance to have a chat once Alex had cried himself to sleep.' She raised her brows in a derogatory fashion.

'Don't you think it's okay for men to cry?' I asked.

'What?' She gave me a small frown. 'Of course it is. But I do think Alex is milking it. That sounds really mean, I know. But believe me, if you knew Alex you'd feel the same as I do. That man knows how to manipulate people. Just like Bernice did. Only she was much better at it.'

'Alex was much better at it with women than Bernice was,' Elsie said.

'True.' Josie nodded. 'But here's the problem. We know Diana adored Alex. That he meant the world to her. Until this summer. We were all relieved when she told him to get lost and started divorce proceedings based on his infidelity. But since he's been back at the cottage, I think he's wormed his way back into her heart.'

'Surely not?' Elsie sounded horrified.

'Last night Di told me that Alex has definitely changed. Bernice told him he was being an idiot and to think carefully about what he was throwing away by letting Diana go. He told Di that he'd done exactly what his mum had said and he'd realised she was right. He'd apparently already dumped Marina. In November, so he told Di. Marina didn't take it well, according to Alex, but he said that he wanted to make a fresh start. He'd ended things with Marina in the hope that he and Di could maybe try again. Can you believe that? And Di never said a word to me about that until last night.'

'Really? So when did he say all this to Diana?' Elsie asked.

'Early December. That weekend he came down to see the kids and stayed at the Sunrise B&B. Di even says that shows how much he's changed. The 'old' Alex would've stayed at the Easterhill Hotel and Spa because the 'old' Alex had to stay in luxury hotels, not in a lowly B&B.'

Elsie laughed. 'Don't tell Lilith her B&B is lowly. She'll murder Alex if she hears that. Oh. On second thoughts, do tell Lilith.'

I grinned even though perhaps I shouldn't have.

'Alex likes to be pampered, does he?'

Josie tutted. 'Alex likes to be the centre of the Universe and have everyone running around after him, so yes. And I must admit, even I was a bit surprised when I heard he was staying at the B&B. But I don't believe he's changed. I think Bernice told him to stay there because she knew it would look good.'

'Did Alex really do what his mum told him to?'

'Yes!' Josie and Elsie emphatically agreed.

'Gosh. I can cope with a man in tears – and actually I think it shows strength of character when a man isn't afraid to express his emotions, but a man doing as he's told by his mum once he's past a certain age is a big no-no.'

'Absolutely,' Josie said. 'And that age is eighteen, not getting on for thirty-eight. I think that's why Alex is so upset now. He's so used to Bernice telling him what to do that now she's gone, he's completely and utterly lost. And the point about that is that Diana says this might be the making of him. Bernice dying, I mean. This is awful, isn't it?'

Elsie nodded. 'So she thinks he might become his own man once he grows accustomed to not having Bernice controlling his life?'

'Or,' I said, 'perhaps Diana sees this as an opportunity to take Bernice's place and to start telling her husband what to do.'

Elsie and Josie both looked at me.

'Yes,' Josie said. 'That's what worries me. Because that's almost exactly what Di said to me last night. That perhaps, now that Bernice was gone, Alex might start listening to her and doing what she wanted him to do for a change.'

'Do you think he might?' I asked.

'It's possible I suppose,' Elsie said. 'But can a leopard really change its spots? I know he ended each of his extra-marital affairs as and when Bernice found out about them and told him to, but it didn't deter him from starting a new one a few months later, every time. If

Diana thinks his cheating ways will suddenly stop, she may be in for another disappointment. And what about Mikkel? I thought things were going so well between them.'

'Me too,' Josie said, frowning slightly. 'She says she does love Mikkel. But that Alex has been a part of her life for so many years and even though she thought she would get over him, she's not entirely sure she wants to. Plus, there're the kids to think about.'

'The kids love Mikkel,' Elsie said.

'I know. But they also love their dad, in spite of the fact that he hardly paid them any attention for years. And Orla told me that Becca was telling her that he seems to really need them right now, so even Becca's willing to give him another chance.'

'Do you seriously think Diana will take him back? Is that what you came here to tell me?' Elsie looked shocked.

'Yes.' Josie nodded. 'And to ask for your help in trying to make her see sense. Mum and Dad will be arriving next week, as soon as they get back from their Caribbean cruise, and although they both want her to divorce Alex now that they finally know the truth about him, you also know that Mum would prefer not to have a messy divorce in the family. If she thinks Alex has changed and that there's a chance he and Di could patch things up, she'll be like a tactical missile in trying to make that happen.'

Elsie rolled her eyes. 'Oh good grief, you're right. I'd almost forgotten that Tibby and Tom were coming here for Christmas.'

Josie smiled at me. 'Diana and Alex usually spend Christmas at their ski chalet in France, apart from once or twice when we've gone to their home in Blackheath. Elsie and I only tend to go for the day and only when it's in London. Mum and Dad always spend Christmas with Diana. At least they always had until this year and that's not going to change, no matter what. But this is the first year we'll all be together for the entire festive season, now that I'm living here with Liam. And with Orla, of course.'

She let out another of those sighs and I couldn't help but smile, despite feeling a twinge of envy that both my distant cousins had men in their lives who seemed to love them. Unlike me.

'You love him a lot, don't you?' I said.

'More than I ever thought possible. And I'm not sure who is the most surprised by that fact. Liam, me – or my mum.'

'Tibby, definitely,' Elsie said. 'I think deep down, you and Liam always had feelings for one another, even when you were young. It just took a while for the time to be right for you both.'

'You believe in Fate then?' I wasn't really surprised.

Elsie looked directly at me and there was something odd about that look but I couldn't quite put my finger on it.

'Absolutely. Fate has played a big part in my life. And in the lives of so many people I know. Don't you?'

'I believe that life sends things our way but that it's entirely up to us what we do with those things. I don't believe it's all pre-destined. But I also believe life is chaotic. So many things are out of our control.'

'That's Destiny,' Josie said. 'Fate sounds bleak. Destiny sounds romantic.'

'Destiny or Fate or whatever you want to call it, took Mum and Dad from me. I'm not a fan.'

Once again, the doorbell interrupted us, and this time Merry not only got to her feet and barked loudly, she also turned up her lip and growled, just like she did when Clark came round.

'That must be Diana,' Josie said, leaping up to answer the door.

'Not quite the speed of light but at least she's here.' Elsie glanced at me as Josie left the room. 'Probably best if we don't mention our discussion about Diana and Alex unless Diana brings it up.'

'Of course,' I said. 'I won't say a word.'

Nine

I didn't take to Diana as much as I did to Josie. I don't know why because Diana was extremely friendly, but there was something about her. Something beneath that perfect smile, the immaculate dress sense and the beautifully-styled hair, that I didn't trust. That sounds ridiculous, I know, but whereas I immediately liked Josie, I thought I'd reserve judgement on Diana until I got to know her better.

She was completely different to Elsie and Josie in looks. She was graceful, elegant and petite with hair the colour of dark honey and just a hint of gold, whereas Elsie and Josie seemed more relaxed, both in looks and attitude, I thought.

Even Diana's voice sounded more controlled, as if she considered not just what she was saying but the tone in which she said it.

'I'm delighted to meet you, Lottie, and so happy to have a cousin. Even a distant one, or one by marriage and not by blood. Our dad has no siblings, so there are no cousins on that side of the family, and of course, Elsie, is our mum's only sibling, and as she had no kids, there are no cousins there either. I can't wait to get to know you, and to introduce you to my husband, Alex and our kids, Becca and Toby. And I'm sure Merry and our dog Henry will soon be the best of friends.'

I have to say, Merry clearly felt the same as I did, and wasn't sure about her at all. And she seemed genuinely surprised when Josie told her I was staying at the B&B.

'Why on earth would you do that? Elsie has plenty of room but if you'd rather stay with someone closer to your own age, then do please come and stay with us at Sea View Cottage. My husband is staying. That sounds strange, but we've been going through a rough patch and have been living apart for a few months. Mum and Dad will be arriving next week, and I must warn you, Mum's a bit of a ... let's just say, Mum can be difficult. Becca's boyfriend, Noah may be staying with us for a day or two, or with his aunt at Seahorse Harbour Holiday Park. But even so, there's still plenty of room. It's a spacious cottage. In fact, it's not really a cottage at all.'

'Oh God,' Josie said. 'Mum's a nightmare. Don't put yourself through that unless you're a glutton for punishment. I can ask Liam if you can stay with us if you really don't want to stay here. But Elsie's fantastic so why wouldn't you?'

I smiled gratefully. 'Thanks for the offers, but as I've already explained to Elsie, we're happy at the B&B and I don't want to leave Lilith in the lurch.'

'But you're family,' Diana said, sounding rather put out. 'At least you are now.'

Elsie tutted but it was followed by a laugh. 'Leave Lottie alone. I've already told her there's no pressure and she knows she's more than welcome here. Now she also knows she's welcome at your homes too. But if she's happy where she is, then that's fine. She's only met me a few times, and the two of you, just now, so it might be a bit overwhelming for her to jump right in. There's plenty of time for us to get to know one another.'

Diana didn't look convinced but she smiled. 'Let's go out to lunch. My treat. I've got some news.'

'It's only just gone 10 so it's a bit early, isn't it?' Josie said, grinning at her sister.

'Oh. It seemed much later. But I've been up half the night. I don't know if they mentioned it, Lottie but my mother-in-law was cremated yesterday and my husband is beside himself with grief. They were very close.'

Josie cleared her throat and gave Diana an odd look.

'Joined at the hip, you mean.'

'I'm sorry for your loss,' I said. 'I had heard the sad news and I arrived just as the funeral started. A lot of people attended so she must've been well thought of.'

'I think they wanted to be sure she was gone,' Josie said. 'Personally, I couldn't abide the woman.'

Diana scowled at her.

'Be nice, Josie. The poor woman is dead. She may not have been the easiest person to like but she didn't deserve to die the way she did.'

'That's true.'

'It was a hit and run, I understand.' I gave Diana a sympathetic smile. 'Do the police have any idea who did it? Were there cameras in the vicinity?'

'Sadly not. But they said they are pursuing enquiries, whatever that means. Alex doesn't think we'll ever find out. Which is probably just as well in a way. He'd kill them if he could and that's not a good attitude for a highly successful heart surgeon to have, whose sole purpose is to save lives.'

The doorbell rang again. Merry barked and Elsie shook her head.

'It's like Piccadilly Circus today.' She laughed as she stopped in the doorway. 'Can you hear carol singers? Or do I need to get my hearing checked? I turned off the radio so I know it's not that.'

Josie laughed too. 'It's carol singers. 'Tis the season, after all.'

'Where did I put my handbag?' Elsie glanced around the room.

'It's in the hall on the stairs,' Josie said. 'I spotted it when I arrived. Shall I go and pay them?'

'Would you, honey bee? Thank you. Give them a tenner. That should keep them quiet.'

'Don't you like carol singers?' I asked her, as Merry began to join in. 'Shush, Merry.'

Elsie laughed louder. 'Merry sounds more tuneful than they do. Why do people who can't sing always think they can?'

'That reminds me,' Diana said. 'I saw Perse on my way here. She's the vicar of St Mary Star of the Sea, Lottie. Her name's Persephone but everyone calls her Perse, which is pronounced like the man's name, Percy but is spelt with an 'se' on the end and not a 'cy'. Don't make that mistake if you send her a Christmas card or you'll never hear the last of it. For someone whose business is forgiveness, she's not very forgiving if you misspell her name.'

'Is that your news?' Josie said, returning from the front door. 'That you saw Perse this morning.'

She grinned and nudged her sister and I could see that despite their banter, they were very close. It must be lovely to have a sister to confide in. Or even a brother. But at least I had cousins, albeit distant cousins, whom I'd finally met after all this time.

'Yes,' Diana replied. 'Because seeing the vicar as I walked past the church is headline news. Of course it isn't. But Perse did remind me that there's a carol concert tomorrow night and she expects us all to be there because naturally, everyone in the village will be attending. That will now include you, Lottie.'

'Tomorrow night? I'd love to go but I can't leave Merry alone in our room. She's settling in but it's still too early to leave her on her own.'

'There's no need to,' Diana said. 'Our vicar is one of a kind. She truly believes we're all God's creatures and is happy for anyone to take their pets to church. We've not only had cats, dogs and rabbits, we've had sheep, goats, tortoises, even a snake. That caused quite a stir, especially when someone asked if the snake had brought an apple to tempt us all.'

'I missed that one, sadly,' Elsie said to me. 'I only go to church for funerals, weddings, christenings and at Christmas. But the carol concert's a must and we all go to that. Then there's the Meet and Mingle Jingle afterwards which is fun. It's basically a Christmas buffet for which everyone pays a fiver and provides a dish or two for the table. It's a chance for everyone to chat and there's even mulled wine.'

'The Meet and Mingle Jingle,' I repeated. 'I

like the sound of that. But why 'Jingle'? Is there music? Or more singing? Or is it just because it's Christmas?'

'No.' Diana grinned. 'It was just the Meet and Mingle when Perse planned it, as a way for her to get to know the residents and for them to get to know her and others they might not have spoken to very often. But one or two of the villagers had a bit too much mulled wine and went into the belfry and rang the bells. They didn't know how to, so people were swinging all over the place. Someone even got his foot caught in one of the bell ropes and was swinging there the entire evening. He was fine, don't worry. So the next year, Perse added the 'Jingle' and now anyone who wants to have a go at bellringing can do so, with supervision.'

'Afterwards,' Elsie added, grinning, 'a few of us adjourn to the pub and this year the plan is to continue on to Neptune's Nightclub.'

'I've never been,' Josie said. 'I'm really looking forward to it. This'll be my first Christmas in Seahorse Harbour in years. Half the collection from the Meet and Mingle Jingle goes to The Seahorse Riders to help with conservation of the seahorse population, so it's for a good cause.'

'Are pets also welcome to that?'

'Yes,' Diana said. 'If they're well-behaved and looked after by their owners.'

'Merry will be more than welcome,' Elsie

said. 'And some of the pets are better behaved than their owners. Take it from me.'

'Count me in,' I said, already looking forward to it. It would be a great way to meet more of the villagers ... and possibly a chance to see the delectable vet, Asher Bryant, once again.

'So what was your news?' Elsie asked Diana.

I'd forgotten Diana had said she had news to share.

'Ah. Now I don't want you and Josie to get cross because nothing's settled yet and we'll have to see how Christmas goes, but Alex has definitely changed and he really needs me and the kids right now. So ... I think I may give him another chance.'

'What?' Elsie said, glaring at her.

'Are you completely mad?' Josie added, glowering.

'Aren't you seeing someone else?' I asked, although I had no idea why I said anything at all, especially when all eyes turned to me. 'Sorry. It's none of my business. But I think Lilith mentioned you were now seeing Mikkel Meloy. Or did I get that wrong?'

'No.' Josie glowered at Diana again. 'You got that right. What about Mikkel, Di? Does he know about this?'

Diana slowly shook her head. 'Don't shout at me. It's a difficult situation, I'm well aware of that. But I can't help the way I feel. I thought I was over Alex, I really did. But it seems I'm not. Mikkel knows that we've been spending more time together, obviously, and he knows that Alex told me he's given up his cheating ways and wants to try again. But until Bernice's accident, I didn't think I'd ever consider going back to Alex. Since Bernice died, we've talked a lot more. And he realises how much he hurt me. And not just me but also the kids. He's promised me he'll try to be the perfect husband and the perfect dad, if I'll give him another chance. He says he never stopped loving me. Even when he was considering leaving me for Una, he said he knew deep down he never would.'

'Una?' I queried.

'My boyfriend, Liam's late wife,' Josie told me. 'Alex also had an affair with her. It's a long story, so we won't go into that right now. Not until we've beaten some sense into my stupid sister, that is. I can't believe you're even giving this a moment's consideration, Di. The man cheated on you for years. Do you honestly believe that just because his mum is dead, he's completely changed overnight?'

Diana raised her head and stuck out her chin. 'Actually, I do. You've hardly spoken to him other than to give him your condolences, but if you did you'd see he's not the man he was. He's deleted a whole list of women's names from his phone. He did that in front of me so I know it's true. And he's added that 'trace my phone app' to his and my phones so that I can see exactly where he is, and if he calls and tells me he's working late, I'll be able to see if he's actually at the hospital.'

'He could get another phone and leave his there,' Josie said. 'And deleting a list of women doesn't mean he hasn't got their numbers elsewhere. Or that he won't start a new list. I'm sorry but I just don't trust him.'

'I know,' Diana said. 'But I told you in the summer that I'd always loved him beyond all reason. I thought I'd broken the hold he had on my heart, but I haven't. This week I've realised that I still love him beyond all reason. I do love Mikkel too, so this is really hard. But I've thought about it a lot this week and I love Alex more. I need to give him another chance. I need to do this for me and for the kids. I want him back. But more importantly, I honestly believe he wants me. And in a way that I don't think he ever really had before. Me telling him to get lost this summer was a real wake-up call for him. Bernice's death has made him realise that we can lose those we love in the blink of an eye. It's made him realise what and who he truly wants. And he wants me, Josie. He really does. I don't expect you to agree with this decision but I know that you and Elsie love me and that you'll support me if this is truly what I want. And it is. It definitely is.'

Josie held her gaze and then glanced at Elsie and at me and she shook her head and sighed.

Elsie stepped forward and took Diana's hands in hers.

'I can't say I agree, but if you want to be with Alex, then of course I'll support you and help in any way I can. Just remember that you're a powerful, beautiful woman, Diana, who can be in control of her own life. Don't let Alex, or anyone else, ever take that away from you again.'

'I won't. Alex knows that if he ever cheats on me again that really will be it and he'll never have another chance, no matter what.'

Josie let out another heavy sigh before smiling at her sister. 'You're mad. But then you've always known that. Of course, I'll support you if this is your choice. But be careful, Di. And this time I'm not stepping in when you tell Mum and Dad.'

'Oh God. I'm not looking forward to that. I might get Alex to do it.' She grinned. 'Sorry about this, Lottie. You must be feeling a bit left out. I should've kept it to myself once I saw you were here, but I couldn't. I needed to tell my sister and my aunt before I tell Mikkel. And I've got to tell Mikkel today. I can't postpone it, unfortunately.'

'I don't envy you that conversation,' I said.

'My boyfriend just dumped me and I have to admit, I didn't take it well. In fact, I behaved rather badly.'

Why on earth had I just told them that? I hadn't meant to. And why were tears pricking at my eyes? Surely I'd cried enough already, hadn't I?

'Oh, sweetheart,' Elsie said, and to my astonishment she dashed to me and pulled me into her arms. 'Why didn't you say something earlier?'

And then Josie and Diana came and joined in the hug and I couldn't hold back the tears any longer. Even Merry nuzzled her way in between us.

I didn't cry for long and it was a truly weird moment but one that filled me with hope and a sort of strength. I felt as if I were a part of this family. Diana and Josie had shared some intimate details of their lives with a complete stranger, and I had shared some of mine with them.

Isn't that what families did?

This Christmas might not be as bad as I'd expected.

'Why don't we have some more hot chocolate?' Elsie suggested, as the four of us and Merry, eased apart. 'Then we'll snuggle up on the sofas and you can tell us all about it. But only if you want to, that is.'

And that's exactly what we did.

Christmas was looking more promising by the minute and with the prospect of the carol concert and the Meet and Mingle Jingle tomorrow night, it might be even better than I'd ever imagined it could be.

Ten

By the time I'd told them what had happened with Clark and me, explained why I no longer had a job, and filled them in on the various mistakes I'd made regarding my living arrangements, it was almost 12 and Diana said that now we could all go for lunch.

'Don't you think you should tell Mikkel that you're breaking up with him and going back with Alex?' Josie asked.

'I'll do that after lunch. I promise. I think I need some wine before I face that awful task.'

Josie frowned at her. 'You've had two of Elsie's hot chocolates. There were at least two measures of brandy in each of those. If you add wine to the mix you'll be too drunk to say anything sensible.'

'Just one glass of wine,' Diana pleaded. 'And I'm hungry, so I need to eat first or my tummy will be growling at him the whole time I'm telling him.'

'What? The three mince pies you've eaten

weren't enough?'

Diana tutted. 'Sometimes you can be such a grouch.'

'And sometimes you can be very selfish, Di. Mikkel loves you. He needs to know that it's over between you two, sooner rather than later. It's not fair to him to delay this. And what if Alex says something to someone and Mikkel finds out that way? He'll be devastated.'

Diana sighed. 'Alex has hardly been outside the house since Bernice's passing. But you're right. I know you are. There's always a chance someone might call round to see him, or telephone to ask if there's anything they can do. It's surprising how kind everyone has been, especially as we all know Bernice wasn't exactly popular. I just ... I don't know what to say to Mikkel or how to break the news as kindly as possible. I really don't want to hurt him.'

'Diana,' Elsie said, with a hint of exasperation, 'Josie is right. You are being selfish. We all know this is difficult but sometimes we need to be cruel to be kind. No amount of alcohol is going to make this easier. Put on your big girl pants and go and tell Mikkel it's over.'

'This is just a suggestion,' I said, 'but we could meet for lunch after you've told him. That way you'll be able to 'drown your sorrows', as the saying goes. Unless Josie and Elsie have other plans.'

'That's an excellent idea,' Josie said.

Elsie nodded in agreement and smiled at me. 'I have no other plans. That sounds like a good idea to me.'

'And me,' Diana added. 'But I'll need about an hour. I can't just walk in and tell him. As much as I wish I could get it over with as quickly as possible. I'll need to sort of build up to it.'

'Be gentle,' Josie said. 'And kind.'

Diana sighed. 'I know this sounds awful but I wish I could have both Alex and Mikkel. They're as different as chalk and cheese and I really do love them both. I just love Alex a little bit more. And the two of us have spent half our lives together, whereas Mikkel and I are still getting to know one another, really. Oh, why is this so hard?'

'Because your life is a bed of roses,' Elsie said, 'and you can't always have roses without any thorns. Now go and tell him.'

'Okay. I'm going.' Diana walked towards the door.

'Er. There's just one thing none of us has considered,' Josie said, and Diana glanced back at us. 'If you tell him now, where are we going to go for lunch? He'll probably still welcome us, but you, Diana – not so much.'

'Ah,' Elsie said. 'Seahorse Bites Café then, I suppose.' She smiled wanly at me. 'Mikkel owns the only pub and the only restaurant in the village.'

'Other than Happy Hot Dogs or Pool Pizzas over at the Seahorse Harbour Holiday Park,' Josie added.

Diana pulled a face. 'Oh Hell! That hadn't even crossed my mind. I was hoping for more than a hot dog or a pizza and as much as Lyn's a great cook, the menu at Seahorse Bites Café isn't brilliant.'

'It's a café,' Josie said. 'It serves homecooked, wholesome food. If you want to eat gourmet dishes, don't break up with Mikkel, break up with Alex.'

Diana looked thoughtful.

'Oh my God!' Josie thumped her on the arm. 'You're not actually reconsidering, are you, based on where you'll have to go for lunch!'

'Ow! That hurt. Of course I'm not. But it is going to be a problem, isn't it? I mean, if Mikkel takes this badly, I won't be able to go to the pub, restaurant or nightclub for a while. And it's Christmas.'

'Diana!' Josie looked cross. 'Perhaps that's something you should've considered before you had an affair with Mikkel. It's too late now.'

'I know. I'm just saying. That's all. We could drive to Easterhill and have lunch at the hotel. Or somewhere in town.'

'Have you seen the weather?' Elsie asked. 'And Josie was right about my hot chocolate, so you're possibly over the limit to drive.'

Everyone fell silent for a moment, except for Merry who made a couple of low, soft barks.

'Um. I think Merry needs to pee. And I really should take her for a short walk. I know the café isn't what you had in mind, Diana, but it welcomes dogs, according to the sign I saw, and it looked cosy, warm and popular, so the food must be good. There's nothing quite like homecooked, wholesome, comfort food after an unpleasant break-up.'

Josie smiled at me. 'Lottie's right, Di. And we can either come back here afterwards and open some wine, or go to Liam's place and do that.' She laughed suddenly. 'I still can't quite get used to saying that it's my place too. But you know what I mean. Orla's out with Darren. He's her boyfriend, Lottie. Liam's at The Olde Forge, slaving away to get some last-minute orders made and sent off by Monday, so he won't be home until about 6 or so.'

'Or we could meet at mine,' Diana said, looking a little more cheerful. 'Alex won't mind, and he promised he'd take Toby sledging this afternoon if the snow kept up, so they'll probably be out. He needs to do something active to help take his mind off what's happened to Bernice. Becca's shopping online, or she was when I left, and she'll probably still be doing so until this evening. You know what teenage girls are like.'

I didn't really, but felt there was no point in saying so. One thing I was sure of was that I definitely liked Josie more than Diana.

'Right,' I said, attaching Merry's lead. 'Merry and I must go out. Shall we meet you at the Seahorse Bites Café around 1 then?'

'I'd like some fresh air,' Elsie said, smiling at me. 'Would you mind if I came with the two of you?'

'Not at all. I thought we might pop down to the beach. The tide was going out when we walked here. I think it still had a way to go but I don't know if it's come back in by now.'

'It should be on the turn,' Josie said, glancing at her watch. 'Yep. Six hours to go out, six hours to come in. Or to be totally accurate six hours, twelve and a half minutes each way, around most of the UK coast, although there are some exceptions. Tides are governed by the lunar day.' She grinned at me. 'Liam's a Seahorse Rider so he knows all about the tides, and since I've been living with him, so do I. Oh. A Seahorse Rider is a volunteer who helps with the conservation of the seahorse population around here.'

'I didn't know about the tides, but I did know about The Seahorse Riders. I read about them on the internet before I came. I met another one yesterday. Asher Bryant, the local vet.' I laughed. 'But of course you know who he is.'

'We know Asher well,' Josie said. 'How did you meet him? I hope it wasn't because Merry needed his services.' She seemed genuinely concerned.

'No. Thank goodness. We went for an evening stroll and Asher was out running. He stopped to chat. Well, he stopped to stroke Merry and then we chatted.'

I could feel my cheeks burning just thinking about last night and that gorgeous smile of his.

'Asher's lovely,' Diana said, still hovering in the doorway.

'And he's single, if you're interested.' Josie winked at me.

Heat rushed up to the roots of my hair. I had to get out of there before they all realised I was halfway to having a crush on Asher already.

'I'll only be here for a week, so I really can't think about romance or anything of the sort. But I must get Merry outside so that she can pee.'

Diana stepped aside and Elsie followed me into the hall.

'I'll get our coats,' she said.

'I'm going to tell Liam what's happening.' Josie grabbed her coat from the chair. 'I know I could text him but I haven't seen him since breakfast and all this talk about men has made me want to go and give him a great big kiss.'

She laughed as she pulled on her coat. 'Come on, Di. You can't put this off any longer. We'll see you at the café.'

We all made our way outside and I couldn't believe how much the weather had changed since I'd gone into Seaside Cottage. A pale lemon sun was now shining, making the snow around us sparkle under its rays. Wisps of light grey clouds scudded across the baby blue sky. But a bank of exceedingly heavy-looking, charcoal coloured clouds sat over the horizon.

'That looks like rain,' I said, nodding towards them.

'Those are nimbostratus,' Josie said, tutting loudly and laughing, as soon as she'd said it. 'God. I even know what all the cloud formations are now, thanks to the love of my life. I'm becoming more like a walking encyclopaedia every single day. Anyway. They could be bringing rain, or more likely, another dump of snow.'

'More snow? Really?'

I had nothing against snow. In fact, I quite liked it and it was lovely to look at, but taking Merry for her walks wasn't quite such fun. Her long fur brushed against it and even with her warm coat, it got onto her fur and formed large clumps of ice.

'Don't you like snow?' Elsie asked. 'Josie and Diana love it. So do I, I suppose.'

'I love it to look at and to build a snowman,

116

or make a snow angel, but Merry's tummy is closer to the ground, so she's not a huge fan.'

Merry barked as if to agree with me.

'Poor Merry,' Elsie said. 'That hadn't occurred to me. Perhaps we should ask one of the men to make her a little sled?'

'But then she wouldn't get to walk, and as a spaniel, she does like her exercise.'

'Sledging is exercise,' Diana said. 'It's really hard work.'

'We should all go sledging,' Josie shrieked, excitedly.

'Not today, honey bee,' Elsie said, as we all gingerly made our way down the sloped driveway.

'Wish me luck then.'

Diana shivered noticeably. Probably more from fear of what she had to do than from the cold.

'Good luck,' the three of us said.

The others gave her a hug, so I did the same, and we all waved as she walked away.

Josie shook her head. 'I feel so sorry for Mikkel. The poor guy doesn't deserve this.'

'I'm surprised Diana is taking Alex back,' Elsie said, a hint of sadness and maybe a touch of doubt in her intonation.

'Me too.' Josie actually looked a little tearful. 'I'm not sure she's made the right choice. No. Scrap that. I'm sure she hasn't. I'll admit Alex does seem to have changed over the last week or so since Bernice died, but once the shock of it wears off, he may well simply revert to his old ways. I heard what she said about the shock making him re-evaluate his life and what's important and all that, but this is Alex we're talking about.'

'I know,' Elsie said. 'But even if we think we know what's best for someone, it doesn't mean we're always right. People do things for all sorts of reasons that we might not agree with, or even begin to understand. That doesn't make them wrong. Every person has to do what feels right for them, no matter what others may say, or think, or feel, or want. And sometimes we have to risk hurting someone even though that's the last thing we want to do.'

Josie glanced at her, raised one brow and cocked her head to one side. 'That's deep, Elsie.' There was a trace of sarcasm in her words.

Elsie cleared her throat, and Merry peed on her garden wall.

'Yes. Well. I think Merry's just shown what she thinks of my pontificating. I should leave sermons to the vicar.'

'And I'll love you and leave you for a while.' Josie grinned and kissed Elsie on the cheek and immediately did the same to me. 'I'll see you in the café.'

We waved her off and crossed the road.

'Let's get Merry to the beach where she can

run around on the sand,' Elsie said.

She seemed to be avoiding eye contact now, almost as if what she'd said a few minutes before had embarrassed her in some way. I didn't know why it should. Her words had made perfect sense to me.

The snow had fallen while the tide was going out so only the sand near the promenade and a few of the rocks were covered in a blanket of white, but the salt air was rapidly eating into that. The rest of the beach was wet sand and looked pretty safe, so I let Merry off the lead as soon as we stepped onto it from the promenade.

She immediately dashed after a seagull that had been bashing a shell against a rock, while another squawked overhead as if warning Merry away, but she bounded forward, regardless.

'She's adorable,' Elsie said. 'And she's grown so big since I last saw her.'

'Yes. She was still a tiny puppy then. But three years is a long time in a dog's life.'

'It's a long time in a human's too, in many ways, but in some, I expect it only seems like yesterday. I wish you'd contacted me before, Lottie. When you were having trouble maintaining the house, I mean. I could've helped you out, financially. You wouldn't have needed to sell. I'd assumed the reason you moved was just because it was too big for one person, or the memories were too much to cope with on a daily basis. I had no idea you moved for financial reasons.'

I lowered my gaze and continued walking, although Elsie had slowed to a stop, but after a few more steps I turned to face her, shaking my head as I did so.

'Mum and Dad left me some money, but I knew if I spent it on the house, it would soon run out, as I didn't have a job. There was no way I would've let you help me out, financially. I hardly knew you. I know Mum and Dad thought the world of you, and that's really one of the reasons I'm here now, but at the time, I sort of resented the fact that you were there and they weren't. That sounds dreadful, but what I mean is that you were always full of life, and Mum and Dad had just died. I know they were both about ten years older than you, but I couldn't help thinking, why them? Why did they have to die?'

'I understand, believe me. When Eric died, I felt the same. Why him? And the strange thing was – and this really does sound dreadful. Far worse than anything you said. I only married Eric to get away from my mum. I'm not saying I didn't love him. I did. But maybe not as much as a woman should love the man she marries. And Mum wasn't a child-beater or anything. In fact, she was a very caring woman. Too caring. She virtually smothered me with her version of motherly love. And she held me up to be some paragon of virtue, which I never was. Not really. I'm five years older than my sister, Tibby, and Mum only wanted one child. She didn't particularly like kids although she'd never admit that to anyone, but to be a real family, one had to have a child, as far as Mum was concerned. Anyway, she made poor Tibby's life a pain by constantly comparing us and telling Tibby she must try to be more like me.'

'Oh gosh,' I said, for want of anything better. I was surprised by this revelation.

'I tried behaving badly, partly to take some of the pressure off Tibby and partly because I was tired of being the 'perfect child', but all that did was upset Mum and make her even more cross with Tibby. When I met Eric it was obvious that he'd fallen for me almost right away. He was kind and considerate. He was everything most women want in a man. In a husband. So I dated him and when he asked me to marry him just a few months later, I said yes without hesitation.'

'Wow. Did your mum like Eric? Was she pleased?'

'She was pleased that he had a career with a bright future, that he was good-looking and polite and that he'd take care of me. Other than that, she didn't say. I felt bad about leaving Tibby, but by then Tibby had learnt to cope with Mum, and she was rebellious and knew how to have fun. You don't know this, obviously, but Tibby has turned into a replica of Mum. A clone almost. She treated Diana like Mum treated me, and Josie, who is younger by five minutes, as a sort of poor second. I was often nagging her about it but she couldn't see what she was doing. And Josie was strong. She is strong. In fact, I think, in a strange way, Josie has actually become a better person. I'm not justifying Tibby's behaviour. But Josie is much more sensitive of people's feelings than Diana is. She's fiercely loyal too. And she's considerate and kind. But for years she was a tearaway and it's only now that she's with Liam that she's really coming into her own and proving what a wonderful woman she truly is.'

'I thought she was your favourite of the two. And I must confess I liked her immediately, whereas Diana, well, I think I need to get to know her a little more.'

Elsie smiled. 'Yes. Diana's lovely, don't get me wrong, but she does take time to get to know and understand.'

'I was so lucky. Mum was the best mum in the world. I know lots of daughters probably say that about their mums, but she really, truly was. And Dad was the best, too.'

Elsie reached out and stroked my cheek with her fingers.

'You're right. You're absolutely right. Lydia

was the perfect mum. The very best. And Russell was the best dad a child could wish for. I completely agree. But it wasn't luck that made them your parents. It was Destiny.'

Elsie believed in Fate. But in my opinion, the difference between luck and Destiny isn't that great, so I wasn't going to argue the point. And when she pulled me close and hugged me tight, I felt we had a bond. A connection. She might not have loved my uncle Eric as much as she should have, but she had clearly loved my parents. And that meant a huge amount to me.

Eleven

Elsie and I sat at one of the tables in the window of Seahorse Bites Café, overlooking the sweep of the bay. Although the notice I'd read stated dogs were welcome, I checked with the owner, Lyn, who Elsie introduced to me, just in case. She didn't seem at all surprised when Elsie told her about our relationship.

'It's lovely to meet you, Lottie,' Lyn said, before smiling down at Merry. 'Dogs are far more welcome than some of the customers I've had in here today. And you my beauty, are better looking than all of them. Yes, you are!'

She had a cheerful smile in spite of her comments about her customers, and her rosy cheeks, soft, warm blue eyes and tight blonde curls atop a body that was a little on the cuddly side, made me think of a cartoon Fairy Godmother in one of my favourite books from my childhood. A book I still owned. Why I'd thought about it at that particular moment, I'm not sure, but even her voice sounded as I'd imagined a Fairy Godmother's would.

'She'll love you forever if you keep that up,' I said, as Lyn tickled Merry behind the ears.

'I wish I could. Sadly, I've got customers to feed.' Lyn smiled and winked at us. 'What can I get you? It's mighty chilly out there, so how about a big bowl of my Christmas chilli?'

'I love chilli!' And I was starting to love Seahorse Harbour. 'But should we wait to order?' I glanced at Elsie.

'Josie and Diana will be joining us, Lyn,' Elsie said. 'We're meeting them here in about fifteen minutes, so would you mind if we wait until they arrive? Or shall we order now so that at least you'll know what we're having?'

'I don't mind either way. What about a nice pot of my Christmas tea while you wait?'

Elsie threw me a questioning look and I nodded, albeit a little hesitantly.

Lyn winked at me. 'It's just regular tea, love, but it comes in a Christmassy pot and with a festive cup and saucer. All handmade by our village potter, the lovely Liam. And I add a tasty little gingerbread man-shaped biscuit.'

I laughed. 'In that case, definitely.'

'Back in a jiffy,' she said, hurrying off.

I told Elsie who Lyn reminded me of and she laughed.

'You should tell her. It'll make her day. She loves to give people advice, and she's extremely kind and generous. She does a lot of work for several charities, including our very own 'Save the Seahorse' campaign. She's certainly a Fairy Godmother to the seahorses. She's brought in several thousands of pounds over the years.'

'Does she run this place on her own? It was packed in here earlier when I glanced in the window.'

Elsie nodded. 'Since her husband died, yes. That was the year before I moved into Seaside Cottage, but I knew him and Lyn from all our years of holidaying here each summer and several other times throughout the years. He was a lovely man. Just like Lyn in many ways. She keeps saying she'll take on some staff but she never has. All her customers are happy to wait when it's busy. Although some of the visitors moan. But only once. She soon tells them they're welcome to leave if they don't like the service. And then she makes them pay upfront before she brings their food, just in case they try to abscond without paying. Two big, beefy guys did that a couple of years ago, but Asher and Liam were here and they soon caught up with them and showed the men the error of their ways.' She laughed, obviously remembering that day.

'What did Asher and Liam do?' I had to ask.

'Not a lot. They didn't need to. It may surprise you to learn that both Asher and Liam have black belts in karate. Not what you expect from a village vet and a ceramicist. The two big guys soon discovered that size doesn't actually matter and that it really is what you do with it, in a manner of speaking.'

Asher had definitely looked extremely fit last night. In more ways than one.

Josie tapped on the window and made me jump. For a second, I was daydreaming about last night. A moment later she burst in, red-faced and beaming.

'She's not back yet then?'

'No.' Elsie gave her a curious look. 'Did you run here, honey bee?'

Josie beamed even more. 'Er. No. Let's just say that Liam may have to stay a little longer to finish those orders this evening. And as I was the one who caused the delay, I may have to go and help him.'

Elsie sighed and fluttered her eyelashes. 'Ah, young love. I remember it well.'

Josie took off her coat and sat beside Elsie.

'Speaking of love, Elsie, is Gray still coming back for Christmas?'

Elsie shot a look at me. 'I believe so. I think he's arriving during the week. But the only love is between him and his son, so don't you go getting any ideas.'

'That's Mikkel's dad,' Josie informed me, grinning. 'Elsie and Gray became very close this summer. She's going to Hell with him in January.'

'That's a real place,' Elsie said. 'It's in Norway and it's where he lives and where Mikkel comes from. And the only reason I'm going with him is so that I can have my photo taken in Hell when it freezes over. It's not because of any supposed romance between me and Gray.'

'Yeah, yeah,' Josie said. 'He's gorgeous. For an older man. But the thing that's just occurred to me and the reason I asked, was because the timing's perfect. Gray and Mikkel get on so well and if anyone can help Mikkel get through this break-up with Di, his dad can.'

'That's a good point,' Elsie said. 'I do hope Diana's been sensible and told him that's it's definitely over. I hope she hasn't left him with any hope that she might change her mind.'

'Here she is,' I said, spotting her walking towards the café.

She burst through the door and slumped onto the chair beside me.

'Oh my God. I really need a drink! That was the most painful thing I've ever had to do. Apart from give birth. Twice. I thought my heart would break.'

'But you did it?' Elsie asked. 'You told him it was over?'

'Yes. But I explained how hard it was for me and how I wished I didn't have to choose.'

'Diana!' Josie snapped. 'What about how hard it was for him to hear it?'

'I said that too. I told him I knew it must be hurting him to know it was over between us, and how that was the last thing I wanted to do. I said how sorry I was. But I pointed out that it was better to find out now, that I was still in love with Alex and that he should think about how much worse it could've been if this had happened later.'

'How did he take it?' I asked, thinking that Diana hadn't exactly been tactful, and remembering how I had behaved when Clark had told me. Although that was mainly because he left me with the bill and without a job.

'Surprisingly well.'

She looked a little disappointed, but I'm sure she wasn't.

'What did he say?' Josie asked.

'He said that he had half expected it after what had happened to Bernice. That he understood how much Alex needed me right now, and that it could well have shocked Alex into changing his ways. He told me it was breaking his heart to hear that it was over between us but that he agreed it was better that it happened now and not in a year or two by which time we might have taken our relationship further, because then it might have been even harder for me. That was thoughtful of him, wasn't it? And then he wished us both well and said he really hoped that this time, Alex would make me happy.'

'Wow!' I said. 'I wish I'd behaved like that. He sounds very calm and collected.'

'He was. And when I told him that we were all meeting here because we didn't think it was appropriate for us – well me – to go to his restaurant, he said I mustn't give that a second thought. I'll be welcome there anytime. We all will. Including Alex.'

'He said that?' Josie seemed surprised. 'I don't think I could cope if someone I loved kept coming to my place of work, especially if they came with their other half.'

'Nor could I,' I agreed.

'I suppose it depends on one's character,' Elsie said, looking thoughtful.

'And how much you loved that person,' Josie added. 'I couldn't come back here for years because of my lost love.' She threw Diana an odd look and Diana lowered her eyes. 'But maybe if I had, it wouldn't have been as bad as I'd imagined. Perhaps Mikkel knows that he can cope with it. That he can handle his feelings. Some men are very good at that.'

'Some women are too,' Elsie said. 'If you know that what is happening is for the best, then you have to suck up the pain and heartache and just get on with your life.'

'Easier said than done,' Josie said. 'I hope he meets someone else soon and falls in love. He's such a lovely guy. He deserves to be happy.' She glanced in my direction. 'What type of guy do you go for, Lottie?'

'I think Lottie may already have her eye on someone,' Elsie said.

'Oh yeah. Asher. I forgot about him.'

'Hello, loves,' Lyn said, approaching our table with a tray, a pile of cups and saucers and a very festive red teapot with large holly leaves and a robin painted on it. 'Here's your Christmas tea. I made a bigger pot and brought extra cups when I saw Josie and Diana. Let me know when you're ready to order. You're both looking well. And how's our lovely Liam?'

'He's even more lovely than ever,' Josie said, stroking one of the cups. 'Liam made these, Lottie.'

'I've told her, love,' Lyn said, grinning. 'And how's poor Alex?'

'Surviving,' Diana said. 'But now the funeral's over we're hoping he'll feel a little better each day. Grief is such a terrible thing.'

'Tell me about it, love.' Lyn shook her head and patted Diana on the shoulder.

'I wish someone would invent one of those memory erasing things so that we could block out pain,' Diana added.

'They have,' said Josie. 'It's called alcohol. But it doesn't last for long.'

Diana frowned at her. 'And as this is a café and doesn't serve any, that's not a lot of help, is it?'

'Ah.' Lyn glanced around and leant in

closer. 'It's not on the menu but it just so happens that I made a batch of my Christmas milkshake again this year, if you'd like a glass of that.'

'Milkshake?' I queried.

What had milkshake got to do with alcohol?

Elsie grinned at me. 'It's not a milkshake, it's a cocktail and it's as alcoholic as my hot chocolate. It's a cross between Bailey's and egg-nog and Lyn makes it to an old, family recipe. It's rich, creamy and rather delicious and more than one will knock your socks off.'

'And it comes in a Christmassy glass,' Lyn said.

Twelve

I've never been drunk on hot chocolate and milkshake before, but by the time we left the café I was feeling a little unsteady on my feet. The Christmas chilli was delicious and I wasn't as surprised as I would've been before I came to Seahorse Harbour, to hear that it contained sherry and dark chocolate. If that was Lyn's idea of home cooking, I'd be happy to live in her home.

Diana invited us back to Sea View Cottage for a glass or two of wine, but I said I had a bit of a headache coming on.

'As much as I can't wait to meet Alex and your kids, I think I've had a bit too much alcohol today as it is,' I said, smiling at her. 'May I take a rain check?'

'Of course.' She seemed a little disappointed. 'You're welcome anytime.'

'And I've got to go and help Liam,' Josie added, 'after delaying his work schedule earlier.'

Her cheeks flushed as she said it. Clearly they'd been having sex. I must confess I had a twinge of envy.

Not that I'd seen Liam, and it had nothing to do with him, but Clark and I had been broken up for a week now and I was beginning to miss the sex. Clark might not have been able to read my mind when it came to what I wanted from our relationship, but he did seem to be able to do that to a certain extent when it came to sex. I wouldn't say he left me completely satisfied every time, but eight out of ten wasn't bad. And even if sometimes it was over merely minutes after it began, all in all I hadn't had much to complain about.

Elsie offered to walk with me to the Sunrise B&B but I told her I'd be fine, and those clouds we'd seen sitting on the horizon had moved closer and grown darker. Either we were in for a bout of torrential rain, or a very heavy snowfall. I didn't want her to have to walk back home in either.

'It's only a few minutes up the road,' I said, as we all hugged goodbye opposite her cottage.

'If those clouds hold off and it doesn't rain or snow,' Josie said, 'we could all meet for a drink in the pub this evening. Although perhaps it's a bit unfeeling to go there straight away, even though Mikkel said he didn't mind.'

No sooner had she said it than the clouds rolled in as if they were on skates. The wind suddenly whipped up and within a matter of seconds, hailstones the size of cherries pounded down on us.

'Come back to mine,' Elsie offered, and we all ran across the road without looking.

I saw the car just as Merry barked and thankfully I was able to tug her out of harm's way as the vehicle skidded on an icy patch in the road but I tripped and fell and as I hugged Merry tight the car kept coming towards us, the driver obviously unable to control the skid in the melting snow, ice and hail.

Strong arms and hands yanked us both out of the way and the car crashed into Elsie's front garden wall, missing us by inches as it swept past us.

The hail stopped as quickly as it had started and I heard muffled screams followed by Elsie screeching, 'Thank God!'

I looked up at the person who had rescued Merry and me, and Asher Bryant was staring into my eyes.

'You nearly got yourselves killed.' He sounded cross and relieved at the same time as his hair dripped water onto me. 'Even in a sleepy village you need to look both ways before you cross the road. And in weather like this you need to be extra careful. Are you okay?'

I couldn't find my voice so I nodded several times before glancing at Merry to check she was unhurt. She was looking up at me as if to ask what had just happened. I don't think her paws touched the ground when Asher grabbed us.

Asher turned his attention to the others but he still held me in his arms. Not close to him, like an embrace, but in a firm hold as if to make sure I didn't go anywhere.

'Elsie? Are you okay? And you two?'

He glared at Josie and Diana who nodded sheepishly.

'We're fine,' Elsie said. 'A bit shocked but okay.'

He glanced at the car but the driver was getting out, miraculously unharmed, it seemed.

'Are you okay?' Asher asked him.

'Yeah. You all right? That was bloody close. I hit the ice before I saw you all. There was nothing I could do.'

'We're all fine, thanks,' Asher reassured him. 'Do you have a phone? Your car won't be drivable.'

'Yeah. My mobile's in the car. I'd better tell the owner of this place that I've damaged their wall.'

'I'm the owner,' Elsie said. 'And don't worry about the wall. It's just bricks and mortar.'

'Don't want it to fall on someone though,' the driver said, scratching his head as if unsure what to do next.

Asher shook his head. 'It doesn't look badly

damaged. I don't think it'll collapse. But it's difficult to tell with all the snow. We'll get a friend to look at it.'

'I'll give you my insurance details, just in case,' the driver said.

Elsie smiled at him. 'It's Christmas. Let's not worry about a garden wall.'

He smiled back. 'Thanks. But how do you know I'm not one of those scammers and that I'll make a claim against you?'

'Oh, I didn't think of that. You look trustworthy and I'm a good judge of character.' She gave him a very smile and a wink.

'I am trustworthy,' he replied. 'I'd better call the breakdown company, I suppose. And my wife. She'll be pleased.'

'She'll be pleased you're safe and so is everyone else,' Elsie pointed out. 'You're welcome to come in and wait. Just ring the doorbell when you've got what you need from your car. We're all soaked so we'd better get in the warm.'

But none of us moved.

'I need a drink to calm my nerves,' Diana said. 'Alex has just lost his mum in a hit and run. Imagine how he'd have felt if I'd been run down too.'

'Lottie is the one who would've been hit,' Asher said with a definite edge to his tone. 'And Merry. And I think you've probably have enough to drink, haven't you? None of you were walking straight and I can smell the brandy on your breath.' He met my eyes and held my gaze.

'But we've only had hot chocolates and milkshakes,' I said, grinning in spite of the situation and not really sure why, but pleased that he was holding me tight.

'Hmm. I suspect Elsie made the hot chocolate and as I saw you come out of the Seahorse Bites Café, I know who made the milkshakes. I realise it's Christmas and there's nothing wrong with getting into the Christmas spirit, literally and figuratively, but for heaven's sake, make sure at least one of you is sober enough to keep the rest of you safe.'

'Absolutely,' Elsie said. 'It's entirely my fault.'

'It's mine,' Diana said. 'I was the one who needed alcohol after breaking up with Mikkel.'

'We all drank them,' Josie said. 'We're all to blame.'

'But none of us could've seen the car skidding any sooner,' I added, 'even if we were all as sober as a judge.'

'Wait. What?'

Asher turned to look at Diana, releasing his hold on me as he did, but when I began to stumble, he wrapped an arm around my shoulder and held me to him.

'Thanks,' I said, as Merry flopped onto my boots and stared up at us.

'You're welcome.' He shot a quick glance at me before staring at Diana. 'Did you just say you and Mikkel have broken up?'

'Yes, I ... Alex and I are giving our marriage another go.'

'You are? Really?'

'Yessss.' She hissed the word as if warning him not to say anything bad about Alex, or to question her decision further.

'Ok-ay. If that's what'll make you happy.'

'It is and it will.'

Asher glanced over his shoulder towards the pub.

'How's Mikkel?'

'He seems fine. He even wished us well.'

'Let's discuss this inside,' Elsie said. 'It's freezing out here.'

And this time everyone did move and started to walk up the drive, but although the hail had washed away some of the snow, it had made the path icy and we all started slipping and sliding. It wasn't really that funny, considering what had just happened, but Josie burst out laughing and everyone else did the same as we tried to help one another to take a few steps without falling over. Even Merry was having trouble.

The driver of the car was the one who eventually got us to the front door. He produced a length of rope from his car boot and clipped a pair of metal spiked soles to his boots.

He was obviously well prepared to walk in this weather but not as well prepared to drive. Like a mountaineer, he led the way and he tied the rope to the tall, cast iron boot scrapper and boot stand that was cemented into the ground beside the door of Elsie's cottage. He also held the rope and one by one we made it safely to the top of the drive. Elsie, being the first, opened the front door to let us in. Asher picked up Merry, who licked his face in appreciation, and he carried her under one arm, holding the rope with the other.

'Now I see what people mean about Destiny,' Josie said, smiling at the driver cum mountaineer once we were all inside in the warm. 'We'd never have got up that drive if you hadn't been here to help us. Your accident was meant to happen so that we could get to the front door.'

And even the driver burst out laughing.

Thirteen

'Thanks for walking us home,' I said, feeling a mixture of excitement and embarrassment as Asher and I arrived at the front door of the Sunrise B&B.

'I wanted to be sure you and Merry made it here safely.'

'I think the brush with near death sobered me up.'

'I don't think the car would've killed you. It looked as if it was travelling faster than it actually was and the guy had managed to slow it down a little, but it would definitely have given you some nasty cuts and bruises. Not the sort of thing a girl wants coming up to the festive season of party dresses and such.'

'Er. I haven't brought any party dresses with me, so that wouldn't have been the problem. Expiring on my aunt's doorstep would've been a downer for her and so would having to visit me in hospital, so thanks again for saving us. Merry and I will have to find a way to repay you.'

'I'm just glad I was there. And there's nothing to repay. But would you call me a jerk if I said that a smile from you was repayment enough?'

His eyes danced with mischief and the colour rose in my cheeks.

'No. But I'd book you an appointment for an eye test.'

'Why? You've got a lovely smile. Please don't take this the wrong way, but you have definitely got that smile from your aunt.'

'My aunt?'

'Yes. Elsie. Although I was surprised when Diana said who you were. I hadn't realised that Elsie was the aunt you told me you were visiting. Last night, I just thought you had a great smile. It was only seeing you with Elsie today that made me realise where I'd seen that smile before. But how are you related? I must've missed that bit. I thought Elsie only had one sibling and that is Josie and Diana's mum.'

'No. You've got it wrong. I mean. Yes, that's right. Elsie does only have one sibling. And no. I don't have Elsie's smile. Although they may be similar. Elsie is my aunt by marriage, not by blood, so I can't possibly have any of Elsie's features, smiles, ticks, quirks, attitude, or anything else. Elsie was married to my uncle Eric who sadly died thirty-three years ago, not long before I was born. He was my mum's younger brother so if I look like anyone other than my parents, it would be Uncle Eric, not Aunt Elsie.'

'Oh. I see. Well, people say we all have doppelgangers, don't they? If there are people we look identical to but to whom we're not related in any way, it's no big deal to have the identical smile to someone who is simply a relative by marriage.'

We stood in the doorway for a moment and for some reason both of us glanced up. The breeze must have made us aware of something moving above our heads.

'Mistletoe,' he said. 'Ah. May I change what I said about nothing to repay? What if I asked for a kiss?'

Heat rushed through me like a boiling kettle. I could hardly say no to that, could I? Even if it did sound a bit corny. But corny in a good way. And it was mistletoe. You had to kiss if you stood under mistletoe with someone, or you'd risk bad luck. I'd just had one near miss, I didn't want another.

Not that I needed to find an excuse to want to kiss Asher Bryant. I'd wanted to do that since the moment I laid eyes on him last night.

I took a deep breath and stood up straight while Merry sniffed around our feet, not showing any signs of impatience to go inside.

'As it's tradition, I can't object to that, can

I?'

He tilted his head slightly to one side and gave me a questioning look.

'You could. If you really can't bear the prospect of kissing me. But would it be so bad? Or do you have a boyfriend and don't like the idea of kissing another man, however innocent the kiss might be?'

'No boyfriend, no. And it wouldn't be bad. Kissing you, that is. I think it would be lovely. No. What I meant was, I really don't mind at all.'

He moved closer and I got nervous.

'As it's Christmas,' I said, just as his lips hovered over mine.

He grinned and tried again.

'And a tradition,' I blurted out.

He backed away a fraction, smiled and moved in for another attempt.

'And bad luck not to.'

He gave a small sigh but remained where he was.

'Sorry,' I said, glancing into his eyes.

He held my gaze for a moment and then he slid his arms around my waist, pulled me against him and kissed me full on the lips.

This was no quick kiss under the mistletoe. This was a proper kiss. A real kiss. A kiss to...

Oh.

My.

God.

This kiss was something else.

Something I had never experienced before.

As he deepened the kiss, I completely forgot where I was, other than in the arms of a gorgeous man whose kiss was sending a wake-up call to every inch of my body.

And after that kiss, Asher looked at me in a way that told me he had also experienced something during it, but I had no idea if it was something good or something not so good.

'I ... I'd better go,' he said. 'I've got a surgery this evening between 5 and 7 and it's...' he glanced at his watch. 'Later than I thought. Er. I hope I'll see you again. No. I mean, I will see you again. Soon. Er. Bye then.'

'Bye, Asher,' I whispered, struggling to speak at all.

'Bye, Lottie.' His head moved closer and I was sure he was going to kiss me again but then it shot back as if it were attached to a string and some puppeteer was pulling it. 'Er.' He ran a hand through his hair. 'Bye. I'll see you around.'

Merry barked, no doubt feeling left out and Asher bent down and stroked her.

'I'll be at the Meet and Mingle Jingle tomorrow night,' I said. 'Are you going?'

I tried to sound as if it was no big deal either way but I think he knew it was. He looked up at me and met my eyes.

'Yes. Definitely. I'll see you tomorrow then,

gorgeous.'

I wasn't sure if he was talking to Merry or to me but as I watched him walk away, he turned around, a huge smile on his face, and waved whilst my heart did an outrageous dance. If it had been wearing a dress it would've tossed the skirt of it in the air like those can-can dancers, and shown everyone its knickers.

But hearts don't do that, do they?

Fourteen

Merry and I had a little nap – at least Merry did; I spent an hour tossing and turning and lying on my back and kicking my legs and feet in the air while pulling silly faces and shrieking with joy. That kiss had caused some sort of temporary insanity, or overwhelming exhilaration, and all I could think about was Asher and the feel of his lips on mine.

Was Asher feeling the same?

Somehow I couldn't see him rolling around on his bed behaving like a lunatic, but I could imagine him rolling around on his bed with me. That made me shriek even louder and wave my legs about even more.

I clearly had a bit more than a crush on Asher Bryant and I couldn't wait to see him again.

I did eventually nod off but my mobile rang and woke me and I foolishly hoped it might be Asher calling even though I knew he didn't have my number.

It wasn't Asher; it was Josie, and she invited me round for a drink and some supper at 8 that evening.

I glanced at my watch and saw it was already 6.30 so I dragged myself off the bed and into the shower, leaving Merry fast asleep with her paws twitching as if she too was having some wonderful dream. Although probably not about Asher.

I met Lilith on my way out and told her where Merry and I were going.

'I'm sure you'll have a jolly time. Josie and Liam are lovely, and so is Orla. Will Diana and Alex be there? Now I'm not one to gossip, as you know, but I heard that Diana has ended things with Mikkel and is giving gorgeous Alex another chance. I'm not sure that's a wise decision but only time will tell. And who can blame her? He is the father of her children, and now that Bernice is gone, Alex will be a millionaire.'

I was walking towards the door as Lilith was speaking, in the hope I could leave before she said too much and I said anything I might regret. I'd only known Diana for one day and I hadn't warmed to her as much as I had to Josie but even so, she now seemed like a relative and a friend and I felt a little protective of her privacy, but I must admit, when Lilith mentioned the word 'millionaire' I did stop momentarily.

'A millionaire?'

Lilith continued: 'Oh yes. A millionaire. He's quite well off in his own right, of course, being such a successful surgeon but Bernice won the Lottery several years ago and was absolutely loaded. Alex is her only child and she adored him, so the money will all go to him. Bernice wasn't one to give to charity or good causes, although they did pay for half of the hospital wing to be built. But that was so that it would be named after Alex. She was very proud of that.'

'She had good reason to be proud of Alex because of his work,' I said, smiling warmly. I liked Lilith very much but I didn't want to gossip about people I now considered as family, especially as they had all made me feel so welcome. 'I don't think we'll be late. I hope you have a good evening.'

'You too, dear. And if lovely Asher walks you home don't stand out in the cold too long. It's bitter out there tonight.'

She smiled and winked at me and I wondered if she'd seen me and Asher kissing earlier. Surely she would've said more than that if she had? Or perhaps she had said more – to other people.

'Asher won't be there,' I said. 'But Merry and I are wrapped up warmly so we should be fine. Good night, Lilith.'

I closed the front door behind me and

beamed, relishing the memory as I stood exactly where I had stood with Asher just a few hours earlier. I quickly pulled myself together and Merry and I carefully made our way down Seahorse Cliffs road, into the village.

Lilith was right. It was bitterly cold, and the snow and hail residues were rapidly turning into a sheet of ice. I could see from the smattering of brown and grey that the gritter lorries had been out, so at least the roads were relatively safe. But after our experience I was a little wary of getting too close to the road.

I was thankful when we reached the patch of open ground so that we could keep our distance. The snow here was still about an inch deep but it scrunched underfoot and was turning icy.

The snow-people Asher and I had passed that afternoon were standing proud, but now there was no sign of the joyful children and no snowballs flying in my direction as there had been earlier. Asher and I had joined in for a short while and we'd laughed like children as we gathered up handfuls of snow and tossed them at the kids and at one another.

I had thought this Christmas would be miserable and that coming to see Aunt Elsie was my chance for one bright spot, but I couldn't have been more wrong. I'd only been in Seahorse Harbour for one day and night and I'd already had more fun and laughed more than I had done in several months.

When had Clark and I stopped having fun together?

Had we ever really had fun?

We'd never had a snowball fight, not even in the first month we were together, and I remembered that it had snowed that December.

But we had been happy, hadn't we?

I struggled to recall the last time we had laughed together. Really laughed. The sort of laugh that makes your belly ache as mine had today, more than once. I genuinely couldn't remember.

I pulled my scarf tighter and blew out a mist of warm air. It was too cold to snow, I was pretty sure of that. I could hear the sea rushing towards the cliffs but other than that it was silent all around us. Lights were shining in all the cottages so everyone was tucked up warmly indoors and the lights in the shop windows on Church Row glowed brightly as we walked past.

There were lights on in the church and soft, mellow strains of organ music filtered out via the stained-glass windows and closed doors. I loved the sound of organ pipes but I doubted they were real in a church as small as this. Several churches used pre-recorded music, or so I heard. I hadn't been to church since Dad's funeral and they'd used recorded music at that. Whatever it was, it sounded wonderful and I recognised the melody of *Silent Night*.

It was certainly a silent night. I seemed to be the only person about. Didn't anyone else in the village have a dog to walk? I know Diana had a dog and I'm sure there must've been others but since I'd left the B&B I hadn't seen another living soul.

It reminded me of the time I'd lived in that thatched cottage in the country. But that had been at least three miles from the nearest village. At least here there were several cottages and a few shops; a pub, a restaurant and a nightclub. Not forgetting the Seahorse Bites Café and of course the Seahorse Harbour Holiday Park which I must go and take a look at during my stay.

And I must visit the sea life centre, not just for a chance to see Asher, but also because I'd like to learn more about the seahorses and why this village worked so hard to save them.

I walked past the ancient oak tree and the bench and heard Christmas music emanating from the pub across the road, along with a muted cacophony of cheery voices. Was Mikkel in his pub, putting on a brave face for his clientele? Or did he have staff so that he didn't have to show himself unless he chose to?

I crossed Church Hill, remembering to look both ways, and smiled at Asher's cottage. Why did a man live in a soft-pink painted cottage? Most men would've wanted to change the colour of the frontage as soon as they moved in. Perhaps there was some by-law in the village that dictated the colours couldn't be changed.

What was it like inside? Was it charming and shabby chic like Elsie's? It was about the same size, but I knew that Asher ran his veterinary practice from there. Josie had told me there was a separate entrance at the side, on Church Hill. I could see the sign and the door as I approached. His front door was on Rope Way and his garden backed onto Wood Lane, which was where I was headed.

Fulbright Ceramics which was situated in The Olde Forge and was Liam's pottery, looked impressive and I made a mental note to take a look inside the next time it was open. I loved the festive crockery Lyn used at the Seahorse Bites Café and I'd seen some of Liam's other work on the internet when I was checking out the village, but, of course, I hadn't realised then that he was Josephine Parnell's partner.

The Olde Forge was at one end of Wood Lane and was once exactly that – an old forge. Liam and Josie's home was in the middle of Wood Lane although strictly speaking it was the last cottage on the lane, but the road continued down towards the promenade. Seaside Cottage, Elsie's home stood on a plot at the end of what was once part of the shoreline cliffs.

The Fulbright home looked exceedingly festive. Was that Liam's doing or Josie's, or a combination of both? There were lights at all the windows in the deep blue façade, and more around the bright red front door. A massive wreath of spruce, pine cones, large red roses, sprigs of holly and mistletoe all tied up with at least two rolls of colourful ribbon and threaded with warm white lights, hung from just below the beard of a wrought iron face of Father Christmas. I could see a large Christmas tree in one window, decorations dripping from every branch and a huge white glowing star sitting at the top.

I rang the doorbell and half expected to hear the Christmas music Lilith had, but it was just a single ring and rather loud.

The door swung open and the most beautiful girl I'd ever seen stood smiling at me. She was dressed from head to toe in an elf costume but instead of looking cutely Christmassy, she looked absolutely stunning. I could never pull off an outfit like that but this girl gave it panache.

'Hello. You must be Lottie. I'm Orla. Please don't mention the outfit. I look like a dork, I know. But my boyfriend's mum asked me to help out at a kids' Christmas party today that was being held at the Seahorse Harbour Holiday Park and I've only just got back. Dad wants to take photos.' She rolled her eyes as she stood aside to let me in. 'You know what dads can be like, right? He's so embarrassing sometimes. Let me take your coat. And who is this?' She bent down and petted Merry.

'It's lovely to meet you, Orla. I've heard a lot about you today. You don't look remotely dork-ish, let me assure you. And this is Merry.'

I let go of the lead and took off my coat while Merry wagged her tail so hard that she almost fell over.

'Aww, she's gorgeous. I wish we had a dog. Dad had said we might get one this summer.'

'But you got me instead.' Josie laughed as she walked towards us.

'Yeah,' Orla said, grinning. 'And Dad says we're going to keep you.'

'Even though you're not completely house-trained,' a male voice added, also laughing.

And then I saw Liam and I could see what Josie meant when she told me he was utterly gorgeous. He most definitely was. His hair was a lustrous chocolate-brown and fell in soft, natural waves around a tanned and exceedingly handsome face. His firm jaw held a hint of stubble and when he smiled, his sensuous-looking lips parted to reveal perfect, naturally white teeth, and his dark blue eyes sparkled as if they were sprayed with glitter. He wore jeans and a Christmas T-shirt and had a fantastic body from what I could tell. Although I must confess that Asher's beat Liam's by a

155

fraction.

He made a sound like 'Ouff' as Josie playfully thumped him.

'Not completely house-trained,' she repeated. 'Right. I'll let you cook supper then.'

'Er. I am,' he replied, pulling her to him and kissing her on the lips before turning to me once again. 'Hi, Lottie. I'm Liam. It's so good to meet you. And hello, Merry. I hear you nearly got your tail run over today.'

'It would've been more than her tail if Asher hadn't saved us. It's lovely to meet you too. Thanks for inviting me round.' I handed Josie a box of chocolates. 'I would've brought wine and flowers or something but nothing was open. Oh! I've just realised, The General Store probably was. Sorry, I didn't think of that.'

Josie smiled. 'You didn't need to bring anything, but thanks for these. They look scrumptious. We'll open them later with coffee. And yes, TGS – that's what we call it, will still be open. It doesn't shut till 9 on Saturday and 10 during week days. Only Sunday hours tomorrow, just for future reference. Please come through to the sitting room. And Liam, get back to the kitchen. I don't know. You just can't get the staff these days.'

She laughed as I followed her and Liam along the hall, his arm around Josie's waist. Orla had taken my coat and Merry's lead and hung them on a rack.

'How long are you staying in Seahorse Harbour?' Liam asked, glancing back at me.

'Only a week, unfortunately.'

Orla laughed. 'Josie was only staying for the summer, and she's still here. And we're all very pleased about that.'

'I'm training her well,' Josie said, grabbing Orla and pulling her into a hug.

'Dad? Can we please take those photos so that I can get out of this silly costume?'

'But you look lovely,' Josie said. 'I think you should wear that on Christmas Day.'

Orla raised her brows. 'Great. I'll get one for you and for Dad and we can all wear them.'

'I would,' Liam said, grinning.

'Me too,' said Josie.

Orla rolled her eyes. 'Oh, God. You two are so embarrassing sometimes.'

'I'll get some drinks,' Liam said. 'What would you like, Lottie?'

'I don't mind. But if it's hot chocolate or milkshake, may I have it without the alcohol, please?' I joked.

'A glass without alcohol is an empty glass,' Orla said. 'That's what Elsie says.'

'That's because everything at Elsie's contains alcohol,' Liam remarked, but he was grinning. 'We've got soft drinks if you'd prefer but we've also got some champagne and as this is the first day we've all met, I think it calls for champagne, don't you?'

'Absolutely,' Josie said.

'I'd love a glass of champagne. Thank you.'

I was being honest. I loved champagne. Clark often drank it and I'd acquired a bit of a taste for the stuff. Now I was out of work, I wouldn't be able to buy my own.

I'd liked Josie the moment I met her. I felt the same about Orla and Liam. Elsie had also been invited and as the evening progressed and we ate, drank and laughed, I really felt at home.

'I hope you don't mind that Diana won't be joining us,' Josie had said as she and I sat in the sitting room prior to Elsie's arrival. Liam was in the kitchen and, after having her photo taken several times, Orla had nipped upstairs to change. 'If she'd still been with Mikkel, we would've, but now that she's back with Alex we'll have to see if we can work something out. Liam really doesn't like Alex. I told you briefly that Una, Liam's wife had an affair with Alex. Well, Liam hasn't forgiven him for that, and I completely understand. But he's said that as Diana's my sister, if she stays with Alex, he'll have to find a way to be polite to the man at the very least. With Mum and Dad coming here for the holidays, we need to do something. We can't avoid Alex entirely, as much as I think Liam wishes we could.'

'I shouldn't say this, but I don't like the sound of Alex, and I'm not sure I'm looking forward to meeting him.'

'You'll either love him or hate him. And knowing Alex, you'll probably love him. Everyone does, at first. Especially women. And to be fair, most people do still love him. It's only us who aren't such fans and that's really just because of the way he's treated Diana, although some of us do have other reasons for not liking him quite so much.'

'Like Liam?'

'Yes. For one.'

'Does Asher like him?' I regretted asking that as soon as I'd said it. 'Asher and Liam are friends, aren't they?'

'Yes, they are. Asher's not a huge fan of Alex, but I don't think he actually dislikes him. Although he didn't like the way Alex kept cheating on Di. Asher's sister, Sorcha was married to a guy who cheated. And did a lot more besides that, but I'll let Asher tell you about it. It's not my place to discuss his sister.'

'Oh gosh! That sounds bad. But of course, although I don't think Asher will tell me his sister's life story. I'm only here for a week after all and we've just met a couple of times. I believe his sister and parents are coming here for Christmas, so perhaps I'll get to meet her at least.'

'Sorcha's great. You'll like her. She's about our age too. She does have really bad taste in men though. She came to stay with Asher at Halloween and met a guy who was staying at the Seahorse Harbour Holiday Park. I won't go into details but let's just say, Asher had to have a word with the guy. He's very protective of Sorcha.'

'I got the feeling that Asher was one of those guys who likes to keep people safe. And animals too, obviously, as he's a vet.'

'Yeah. Asher's definitely one of those guys. And so is Liam. I think if Alex does mess up again and hurts Diana in any way with his cheating and his lies, he'll have both Liam and Asher to answer to.'

'It must be nice to have someone who will protect you in that way – a man who'll stand up for you against the world.'

'It is,' Josie said, as she smiled at me. 'And you'll have that one day too. I'm pretty sure of that.'

Fifteen

I hardly slept a wink.

I spent most of the night dreaming about living in Seahorse Harbour but I hadn't seen exactly where I'd lived or if I'd lived with anyone or alone. When I woke up, it made me wonder. I only rented a flat at the moment. I only had to give one month's notice. I didn't have a job, or anyone special to keep me in Reading. I could live anywhere I wanted. I could live in Seahorse Harbour.

But could I? Could I really do that? And were there any properties to rent? I hadn't seen either a 'For Sale' or a 'To Let' sign anywhere. I suppose the estate agents in Easterhill would deal with properties here. Perhaps I should Google some of the property sites? I'd done that when I was researching what I'd find here, so now I might as well use them for the purpose for which they were intended.

Perhaps this was all a bit fast though. I'd only been here for just over a day. The place might seem like Paradise but it must have its faults like everywhere else. There'd been burglaries in the summer. The roads weren't always safe even if there didn't seem to be much traffic on them. The place had cliffs wherever you looked; they weren't good for Merry. But it did have a vet. A rather gorgeous vet.

Which could prove to be another problem. What if we went out or something by some miracle and then it didn't work? Would I still be able to see Asher as a vet and not another love I'd lost? And what if we didn't ever date and instead he married someone else? Would I spend each day pining for what might have been?

Okay. Now I was being silly. But moving somewhere on a whim was not a good idea. Surely my sojourn in the country cottage had taught me that much?

But I would be near family. My family. That's something I never thought I'd have again. Elsie, Josie and Diana had all made me feel so welcome.

But would that welcome wear thin in time? As I always make a point of telling people, Elsie and I are related by marriage, not by blood, and that was the same for me and Josie and Diana.

On the other hand, it would be wonderful to not feel so alone. I had Merry and she made my life joyful in so many ways, but there were limits to that. Conversation was a problem. I'm convinced Merry understands me and I understand her. Most of the time. But meaningful discussions are not high on our agenda.

And being at Josie and Liam's last night had made me realise how much I wanted what they had. I wanted someone special to love and for that someone to love me. I wasn't completely sure I wanted children. I was always torn whenever I thought about that. Part of me yearned for a child of my own and another part cringed at the idea of it.

Shortly before she died, I'd asked Mum if that was normal.

'Do people feel torn about having kids? Did you and Dad?'

'Not us, sweetheart,' she had said, hugging me close. 'We wanted children together from the day we married. But we thought it wasn't meant to be. And then a miracle happened and you came along and we loved you with all our hearts even before you were born. We wanted you so much and we were terrified of losing you. Until the day we brought you home, we couldn't quite believe it. And we thank God and the Universe and Life for giving you to us. But some people don't have that desire. Some people don't want to be mothers. And that's perfectly okay. Just because we're women and we've got wombs, it doesn't mean we will automatically want to bring up a child. The important thing is, you have a choice. This is your life and it's up to you what you do with it. If that means you raise a child, that's wonderful. But if you don't want to do that, that's just as wonderful provided that you're happy.'

It didn't exactly explain why I felt the way I did; the way I still do, but it did make me feel less of a freak for having doubts.

When I was dating Clark, I desperately wanted to get married and have a family but now I think that had more to do with loneliness than with a desire to be with him and to have his child.

But seeing Josie, Liam and Orla laughing and joking and teasing one another, and seeing how much they clearly loved each other, made me want marriage and family in a completely different way. Orla wasn't Josie's and yet if you didn't know they weren't biologically related, you would assume they were. Orla was stunningly beautiful; Josie was really pretty, but she looked nothing like Orla. I could see some of Liam in Orla, but she obviously took after her mum in the looks department.

What they had was a bond. A strong and true and loving bond. A bond that might stretch and be tested at times but one that would never break. I was sure of that the moment I saw the way Josie and Liam looked at one another and the way Orla did too. They loved one another deeply. And yet Josie, who had been friends with Liam long ago, had only come into Orla's life this summer.

Perhaps that's what Destiny was. It brought together people who were the perfect fit. Who were meant to be together, even after years apart. And perhaps some of us used the word Destiny as an excuse for doing things or not doing things we knew deep down were right or wrong, depending on the situation.

Diana was using Destiny as a reason to give Alex another chance. But perhaps Mikkel was her true Destiny and Diana was blinded by fear, or habit, or commitment, or guilt. Only time would tell. And if Mikkel was her Destiny, perhaps, one day, she would realise that. Then again, perhaps she wouldn't. Destiny might exist but we're the ones who make the choices.

Was it my Destiny to come to Seahorse Harbour? Was this where I belonged? Had everything that happened – all those wrong moves and mistakes – happened so that eventually I would come here? Or was I using Destiny as a reason for me to stay?

Merry barked and as I glanced at my watch I saw that once again, it was way past 7 and time for us to get up.

Sixteen

Breakfast was interesting. Lilith knew about the accident and the damage to Elsie's wall; she knew about Diana, Alex and Mikkel and she definitely knew that Asher and I had kissed. She didn't actually say it to me but I could tell from the little things she did say, about Christmas traditions and mistletoe and how wonderful a first kiss could be. I considered telling her just how wonderful it had been but this involved Asher, not just me and I wasn't going to be the one to spread gossip about him.

Luckily, more guests were arriving that morning so Lilith didn't have a lot of time to chat.

'It's a good thing the weather seems to have improved,' I said, attempting to change the subject. 'With all that snow and ice I wondered if people would be able to travel.'

But that might have been a mistake because that returned her thoughts to yesterday's accident.

'Imagine if Diana had been killed,' she said. 'It doesn't bear thinking about. But you'll never guess what. A friend of mine works for the local newspaper in Easterhill. Alex is a big noise in the town and at the golf club and air field there, not to mention the hotel. Naturally, everyone took a great deal of interest in what happened to Bernice.'

She leant forward conspiratorially and glanced around her but as only Merry and I were there, I don't know why she did that.

'Naturally,' I said, finishing my coffee as quickly as I could and almost choking in the process.

'Careful, dear.' She smiled and waited a moment. 'Well. Doreen, my friend, says that the police have got a lead. That's the Metropolitan Police, no doubt, as Bernice was knocked down in London.'

'I think it was in Blackheath, wasn't it? I'm sure Diana told me Bernice was on her way to their house when it happened. According to Alex.'

'Well, yes. Diana was down here at the time. With Mikkel. But the minute Alex called and told her, she was in her car and at that house within a matter of hours. I suppose we should've realised then that she and Alex would reunite. Poor Mikkel. The thing is, dear, Doreen says that she's heard that they've traced the car involved.'

'That's good news. I'm sure Diana and Alex will be relieved that the culprit will be brought to justice. Unless the car was stolen?'

'Not according to Doreen. And she hears all the latest news.'

'Is she a journalist for the paper in Easterhill?'

'Oh no, dear. Much better than that. She's the cleaner.'

'The cleaner? Then how...? Never mind. I'm not sure I want to know. I'd better make a move, or I'll be late. I'm meeting Josie in half an hour.'

I wasn't, but Lilith wouldn't know that. Or perhaps she would?

'Oh. Right you are, dear. You run along. I've got a lot to do myself this morning. I'll let you know if I hear any more from Doreen.'

'Thanks. Have a good day.'

I felt a pang of guilt for lying but I didn't want to listen to more gossip.

Merry and I walked down to the beach. The shops weren't open yet and as it was Sunday they wouldn't open until either 10 or 11 or so. The tide was going out, just as it was the previous day but we were earlier today so it hadn't gone out as far. I found some chunks of rock, some empty shells and best of all some bits of driftwood and I threw the wood for Merry to chase.

'Hey there,' a friendly-sounding male voice

called out. 'The owner of my house might need that for repairs.'

I shaded my eyes from the pale lemon sunshine and saw a tall, agile figure striding towards me, and a Great Dane trotting regally at his side.

'Sorry. What?'

The man nodded towards the driftwood in my hand as he got closer but I could see a broad smile on his rather handsome face. His golden bond hair blew around like sheaths of corn in the light but chilly breeze and his hands were stuffed inside his jacket pockets, his shoulders hunched a fraction as if he were feeling cold.

'The driftwood,' he said, now only a few feet away. 'Don't mind me. It's my way of breaking the ice. And it's pretty icy out here today. But not as bad as yesterday. I thought the world might end.'

'It almost did for me,' I joked. 'You said the owner of your house. Does that mean you rent a place here? Or that you're a visitor?'

'Visitor, sadly. I'm Kev and I'm staying in The Boathouse.' He nodded back towards the promenade.

'Oh wow!' I replied. 'I wanted to stay there but it was booked. I'm Lottie and I'm staying at the Sunrise B&B up there.' I pointed up towards Rock Road which was just visible from where we stood.

'Hmm. The Sunrise B&B was full at the

time I looked at it in October. The Boathouse wasn't. The owner told me he had only just decided to rent it out and it had just gone live that day. I wish it had been booked when I looked at it. Then I wouldn't have thought it would be the perfect place to bring my girlfriend for the Christmas holidays. Or that a wet and windy beach in the UK in December would be the ideal place to propose. We met on a beach, you see.'

'Oh how romantic. In the UK?'

'No. In Corfu. But the place we met doesn't open at Christmas and my girlfriend's family live in Easterhill so I thought this would be great.'

'Oh dear. I get the feeling your girlfriend didn't agree.'

'She didn't. And she's now my ex-girlfriend. So it's just me and George here. She didn't like the fact I'd brought George either. But you can't leave your dog in kennels over Christmas, can you?'

'Absolutely not. I'm sorry about your girlfriend. But perhaps it wasn't meant to be.'

'You believe in that stuff do you? Destiny, or Fate or whatever.'

'I'm starting to.'

'I'd love to know what it has in store for me and George then. At the moment we're facing the prospect of a cold and lonely Christmas staying in what my girlfriend, sorry, ex-girlfriend, called a beaten up, upturned boat that might blow away at any minute.'

'It looked fantastic in the photos. Don't they reflect reality?'

'I think so. Totally. But she hadn't seen them. She said that if she had she would've disabused me of such an idiotic notion immediately.'

'I think you might be better off without her. Er. You don't seem that upset. Or are you one of those stiff upper lip kind of guys?'

'I think you might be right. George certainly thinks so. Oddly enough I'm not that upset, which is strange considering I was hoping to spend the rest of my life with her. And I'm one of those guys who can cry if my football team loses, so there's nothing stiff about my upper lip. What about you?'

'Similar story. Except my boyfriend dumped me and went skiing with his friends.'

'Nice. Classy fella. And you came here because...?'

'I have ... family here.'

'Lucky you. Our dogs seem to be getting to know one another. Perhaps we should take a leaf out of their book. Unless you have plans with your family?'

He nodded towards George and Merry who were smelling one another's rear ends.

'No plans for this morning. But if you're suggesting we do what George and Merry are doing, then I'm with your girlfriend, I'm afraid. I would need to disabuse you of that notion immediately.'

He grinned at me. 'At least you didn't say it was idiotic.'

I grinned back. 'I think that goes without saying, doesn't it?'

'Probably. What I meant was, would you like to get a cup of coffee? We can go back to my place. Or somewhere else if there's anywhere open.'

'I would like to see inside The Boathouse, but I'm not sure I should go back to your place as we've only just met. You could be an axe murderer who roams the beach looking for lonely women and that story of your girlfriend could all be made up.'

'Good point. I actually wish that were the case. It might be more fun. No. Seriously. It's all true, sadly. And I'm not an axe murderer. If I was going to kill someone I wouldn't use an axe. Far too heavy and cumbersome to carry around. Let's find a café then.'

'Seahorse Bites Café is open. I saw the lights on and a couple of customers going inside as I arrived. The food is delicious if you need a place to eat while you're here, and the owner is lovely. Just don't drink the milkshake. Although as your door is only steps away, it might not be so bad. Sorry. Inside joke. Don't mind me.'

'Are dogs welcome?'

'More so than humans.'

'It sounds perfect. I saw it when we arrived but my girlfriend didn't like the look of it so we went to the pub for lunch and to Hippocampus Restaurant for dinner.'

We began walking towards the promenade.

'Oh wow! What's that like?'

'The food was fantastic and so was the wine. The bill wasn't as bad as it could've been and the service was first rate. It's owned by the guy who owns The Boathouse.'

'Yes. Mikkel Meloy.'

'You know him?'

'No. We've haven't met. But he's ... a friend of my family.'

'Why the hesitation?'

'Er. He and my distant cousin were dating until recently. Until yesterday, in fact, when she ended it.'

'Ah. I know how he feels. There's a lot of that going around.'

Seventeen

Kev and I got on really well. So much so that, when he nipped to the loo in the café, I called Josie and asked if it would be okay if I invited him to the Meet and Mingle Jingle that evening. We'd exchanged numbers yesterday and I thought she was the best person to call. I briefly explained his situation and that he would be coming just as a friend, not as my date or anything, and bringing his dog, George.

'Absolutely,' she said. 'No problem at all. I was just about to call you and ask if you wanted to meet up to go Christmas shopping in Easterhill today. It'll be you, Elsie, me, Orla, Diana and Becca. Diana's driving. The forecast for the next few days sounds horrendous so we decided to get as much shopping done as possible just in case.'

'Oh gosh! Yes please. Er. I know this sounds silly but do you or Liam have any suggestions for something that Kev can do? I think he's a bit shell-shocked to be honest even though he seems fine. I feel a bit guilty to just leave him here on his own.'

'Hold on.' She laughed as she called out to Liam and although I didn't hear what was said, she was still laughing when she spoke to me again. 'Liam says that he and Asher are taking the boat out to check around the bay. If Kev likes inflatables and doesn't get seasick and is happy to help pull rubbish from the sea, he's welcome to join them. They'll find a wetsuit for him.'

'Really? Wow! That's great. Can I have a word with him and call you back? What time is everyone leaving? Us for shopping, them for the sea. Oh. But what about the dogs?'

'Diana's asked Alex and Toby to look after Merry for you. They'll be looking after their dog, Henry, so they were fine with that. I'll call her and ask if they'll look after George as well. What sort of dog is he?'

'A Great Dane.'

Josie laughed. 'Then he and Henry will go well together. Henry's part Great Dane, I think. He's also part horse, part Pointer, part Bloodhound and much more besides, although I've never been sure which part is which. I feel sorry for Merry already. I'll call you back in five minutes. You ask Kev about the sea and I'll ask Di about the dog.'

When I told Kev that I was now going Christmas shopping with my family, which seemed to be a word I couldn't stop saying. Family. It sounded so good. Anyway, he was perfectly happy at the prospect of me leaving him where he was. But when Josie called and said George had a play date with Henry and Merry, and I told Kev that he could go out in an inflatable and that George would be in good hands, Kev looked as if all his Christmases had come at once.

'Really? You're serious? They're happy for me to go with them?'

'Yes. And George will be safe with Alex and Toby.'

As I hadn't met either Alex or Toby I had no idea if that were true, but I trusted Josie and if she thought they'd be fine, I was sure they would.

I told Kev about the Meet and Mingle Jingle and I saw what he meant about not having a stiff upper lip. It actually quivered and I thought he might shed a tear, but thankfully he didn't. I wouldn't have known what to say or do.

'I think I'm starting to see what you meant about Destiny,' he said, beaming at me. 'When I got up this morning I was thoroughly miserable and was facing a pretty depressing day. I'd considered packing up and going home but that would prove my ex had been right and that coming here was a mistake. I knew it wasn't. I can't explain this but it just felt right and that's why I booked The Boathouse. And because of that, I've met you and now this entire day is going to be great.'

I wasn't sure what was so great about sitting in a rubber boat on a grey sea on a chilly day, but at least the sea was calm now, unlike when I first got up. I was sure I'd got the better day ahead though. Christmas shopping in Easterhill with my family was my idea of heaven.

Eighteen

Easterhill, which sits to the north of Seahorse Harbour isn't exactly a metropolis. In fact, it's not even a particularly large town. But it has a shopping centre, a choice of restaurants, cafés and bars, a cinema, a central car park, hairdressers, shoe shops, banks and building societies and all the other shops and businesses you might want.

There's also an air club and a small air strip just outside the town, set on what was once part of the Easterhill Estate. The modest stately home of Easterhill is now a luxury spa and hotel, and the grounds were divided between that and the air club.

Lord Easterhill had a bit of a penchant for planes but when he and his wife died, leaving no heirs, they left the airstrip and the planes to the town of Easterhill and it was turned into an air club. The house itself was sold to a developer and in addition to converting that into the hotel and luxury spa, he eventually obtained permission to use part of the grounds for a golf club.

Apparently, Alex Dunn, Diana's husband was well regarded at the air club and the golf club and hotel. Diana had used that fact more than once to get appointments at the spa even when it was supposedly fully booked. Unbeknown to us when we set off, she had used that connection today. When we were finished with shopping, we had back massages, manicures and pedicures to look forward to.

'I think they've employed extra staff,' Josie said, when Diana told us. 'They only use them when Diana or some other well-connected person calls. Either that or they are nowhere near as popular as they'd like everyone to believe because whenever Di calls, somehow they manage to fit us all in.'

'No wonder you're giving Dad another chance,' Becca joked. 'Who would want to give up such luxury unless they really had no choice?'

I hadn't met Becca until Diana picked up Josie, Orla, Elsie and me from Elsie's house and we all bundled into the people carrier. She was as pleased to meet me as the others had been and unlike her mum, I warmed to her instantly. I don't know what it was about Diana but I couldn't shake the wary feeling I had about her.

I learnt that Becca and Orla were best

friends and Orla was the elder by a year. Orla was also the one who everyone in the shopping centre gawked at. I thought that might make Becca feel a little like she had come second in a beauty contest, but I was surprised and pleased to discover that Noah, Becca's boyfriend had chosen Becca over Orla. Although not so pleased to hear that it had made Orla the one who felt second best. There had been a bit of a falling out over it in the summer but they'd clearly put that behind them because they were like sisters as well as best friends. It did go to prove that beauty is in the eye of the beholder and that gives the rest of us hope, doesn't it?

The shops were full to bursting and Christmas music rang out all around. After a couple of hours shopping, I was counting the minutes until the pampering sessions Diana had arranged. But I got a lot of presents for my family and just having them all to buy for gave me so much pleasure. I had always loved buying presents for Mum and Dad and my friends, but this year it was just my friends, and it hadn't been fun until I'd come to Seahorse Harbour.

We had festive coffees, ate gingerbread men and mince pies, listened to carollers in the town centre, and we even had our photos taken with Father Christmas and a group photo for all of us.

Wherever I might live after this year, I

knew I'd cherish that photo and the memories of the day.

More shopping took us up until lunch and we had Christmas dinner in one of the restaurants. Diana insisted it was her treat. After that we packed in another hour's shopping and then headed to Easterhill Hotel and Spa.

I hadn't even looked at this place when I'd searched for somewhere to stay. There was no way I could afford their prices. But when we arrived and were met by staff holding a tray of glasses filled with champagne and a selection of luxury chocolates, I knew that if I ever had cash to splash this would be where I'd splash it. And once the pampering began in earnest, I wanted to live in Easterhill Hotel and Spa.

I felt like a different woman by the time Diana and the others dropped me at the Sunrise B&B two hours later so that I could put my shopping in my room and get changed. I was to meet them half an hour later at St Mary Star of the Sea for the carol concert, and they'd bring Merry to the church.

It had been a wonderful day and I had treated myself and bought the perfect dress to wear that night. I knew I had to be a little careful with money and I'd spent far more than planned on presents, but I wanted this Christmas to be special and if that meant tightening my belt for the whole of the following year, that was a sacrifice I was willing to make.

I wondered if Merry's day had been as wonderful as mine and I couldn't wait until we were reunited.

Lilith was busy with new guests so I gave her a quick wave as I dashed in and another as I was about to dash out.'

'Lottie?' she called to me as I reached the front door.

'Can't stop, Lilith. I'm meeting everyone at the church and Merry might've been missing me.'

'I won't keep you, dear, but I thought you might like to hear the news.'

'Maybe later?' I suggested.

'It'll only take a second. Now as you know, I'm not one to gossip but we all knew Alex had a string of affairs. But imagine the shock when the police said that the culprit who ran down Bernice and left her crumpled body in the road was one of Alex's *women*.'

I'd almost made it out the door but Lilith knew that would stop me in my tracks.

'What? Are you sure? Is that the truth?'

'As the Lord is my witness, it is. Doreen heard it this afternoon and the police must've informed Alex and the family by now. Doreen wasn't working today as it's Sunday, but she dropped in to the office just to see if there had been any news. She likes to keep abreast of events. I don't know any more than that. Except the woman's name. It's someone called Marina … something. Doreen didn't catch the surname.'

'Marina! I have no idea who that is. Thanks for letting me know. I'll see you later.'

I raced out and closed the door behind me. I didn't want Lilith to realise I'd heard that name before. Only yesterday Diana had told me that Marina was Alex's last affair and that he ended it because Bernice had insisted he did. Had the woman scorned been the woman who had killed Bernice in revenge?

Surely you would have to be out of your mind to do that?

And then I remembered how I had behaved the day Clark had ended things with me. I hadn't killed anyone but I had trashed Clark's desk and accidentally given one of the partners of the business a black eye.

Perhaps it was only a fine line between that and using a car as a weapon to soothe one's anger.

Alex must be feeling even worse if he'd heard that his behaviour had been the catalyst for Bernice's death. I didn't think he'd be attending the carol concert now. And certainly not the Meet and Mingle Jingle.

Nineteen

I tried to call Josie, Elsie and Diana in turn but all three phones were engaged. I didn't want to leave a message because I didn't know what to say. What if Lilith and her friend Doreen had got it wrong?

I waited outside the church, smiling at people as they walked past and went inside. It was certainly true that pets were welcome. So far, I'd seen several dogs, cats, budgies and other caged birds, a rabbit, a hamster, a goat, a pig and something that I wasn't quite sure of and could possibly have been a stuffed toy. Would anyone turn up with a reindeer? It was Christmas, after all.

I tried the phones again but now all three went to their voicemails and I wasn't sure what to do next. Obviously, I was anxious for Diana, who might now be dealing with an even more distraught Alex, but that didn't account for the others. And I was also concerned for Merry. I knew Diana wouldn't let any harm come to her but Merry hadn't seen me all day and she might be getting distressed. I certainly was.

And where was Kev?

Oh God. I hope nothing had happened to him. Or to any of them.

Where was everyone?

And then I remembered that I thought I'd heard sirens wailing while I was getting changed, but they seemed to be in the distance and I hadn't thought anything else of it. But what if something had happened to Diana and Josie and Elsie? What if those sirens had been for them?

No. Now I *was* being ridiculous. They'd only left me about half an hour ago and what could've happened between them dropping me and driving the mile or so home?

Accidents did happen though. Yesterday proved that. And Bernice's death, too. Although clearly that may not have been an accident if what Lilith had told me earlier, was true.

No. I was letting my imagination run away with me.

A slightly overweight woman with short, spiky, white-blonde hair, a purple and gold dress coat and a long flowing purple dress appeared in the doorway of the church. As she approached me, I realised it wasn't a dress she was wearing but her vestments. This must be Persephone, or Perse as I'd been told she liked to be called – the vicar of St Mary Star of the Sea.

'We haven't met,' she said, marching towards me and holding out her hand. 'But the village grapevine has done its job and I know who you are. You're Lottie. Elsie's niece. Am I right? Or am I wrong?'

'You're right. Hello, Perse. It's nice to meet you.'

'Ah. The grapevine has kept you informed too. You know my name. I think I saw you the other day. I called out and said hello and you replied, but I was halfway up a ladder at the time, hanging a few more lights, so I couldn't catch you to properly introduce myself. But why are you standing out here, Lottie? Come inside in the warm. The wind's whipping up a bit and it looks like we'll have rain or snow before the evening's out.'

'Oh. That was you? I ... I thought it might've been a ghost or my imagination. I'm glad to know it was neither. Er. I'm waiting for Elsie, Josie and Diana. I'm supposed to be meeting them here and Diana's bringing back my dog, Merry.'

'Wait in the warm. I'm sure they wouldn't expect you to wait out here. They'll realise where you are.'

'But the problem is, I'm worried they might not be coming. I think ... something may have happened.'

I didn't want to mention anything about Marina and the police. That was Diana's business and I wasn't going to tell anyone, not even a vicar.

'If they said they were, I'm sure they will. Elsie comes every year and so does Diana, when she and the family aren't at their ski chalet. Have you called them?'

'Yes. All their phones were busy and now the calls are going to voicemail. I need to find my dog. She'll be anxious. I need to know what's going on.'

Perse linked her arm through mine and ushered me towards the church door.

'We can find answers to those problems just as easily inside. Come and sit down and we'll put our heads together.'

'But you have the carol concert to deal with. Don't you need to be there?'

'Others can do that just as well as me. Now, have you tried calling Liam, or Mikkel? No, best not call Mikkel at the moment.'

'I don't have Liam's number.'

'I can help with that.'

'Perhaps I should just go to Diana's? Can you tell me where she lives? I haven't been there yet.'

'Lottie!'

I heard a voice I recognised and spun round to see Asher and Kev hurrying towards us, along with Merry and George. Merry's pace increased when she spotted me and it was a good thing Asher was a runner because anyone else might've struggled to keep up with her as she tugged at her lead and raced ahead.

'Asher? Has something happened? Have you seen Elsie, Josie or Diana?'

'Yes,' he said, closing the distance between us.

Merry leapt at me and I bent down and hugged her. Her tail was wagging with excitement and she gave me lots of 'Hello' barks and sloppy kisses.

'I'm glad to see you too, sweetheart,' I said, momentarily forgetting about my aunt and Diana and Josie. 'Yes. I've missed you.'

'Everything okay, Asher?' Perse asked, as Kev and George came and joined us. 'And who might these two lovely gents be?'

'This is Kev and George,' Asher said. 'They're here on holiday. But I need to speak to Lottie, Perse, if that's okay? Although you should hear this too.'

Kev gave me a quick wave of his hand and a wan smile and I could tell by the tone of Asher's voice that something was definitely wrong.

Asher cleared his throat, took me gently by the shoulders, and with Merry's lead hanging from his wrist he looked me in the eye.

'Now I don't want you to panic – and everyone is fine, but they're all at the hospital.

Alex has been hurt. It's not life-threatening but he will be in hospital for several days. And Elsie's got a broken ankle.'

'What? Hurt? Alex and Elsie? How?'

I couldn't believe what I was hearing. I expected him to say that Alex was upset over the latest development in the death of his mum, not that he was in hospital. And Elsie too? It didn't make any sense.

'What happened?' Perse asked, her voice and manner calm and controlled.

Asher shook his head. 'I don't know all the details and it's a bit unclear. All I know for sure is that after dropping Lottie at the B&B, Diana drove Elsie home and then Josie before going to her own home. She was unloading her shopping and Alex had come outside to help when a car raced into the drive and headed directly for Diana. Alex saved her by pushing her out of the way but the car struck him and he's got several broken bones. But as I said, nothing life-threatening.'

'What?' I shrieked. 'How could that happen? I know it's still icy in places but for two cars to skid in just a matter of twenty-four hours? That's unbelievable.'

Asher shook his head. 'The car didn't skid. It was intentional.'

'Good Lord,' Perse said.

'Intentional?' I repeated.

Kev gave me a sympathetic look as if he

didn't know what else to do.

Asher nodded. 'Again, I don't know the details. Diana called Josie, and Liam called me afterwards. Kev and I were in the pub having a quick beer. We met Liam and Josie at Diana's but by then the ambulance had taken Alex and Diana to hospital. Liam and Josie took Toby and Becca, and Orla went with them. We took Merry and George and went back to the pub as there was nothing else we could do. Then I got a call from Liam saying Elsie had taken a tumble and had called Josie but as they were at the hospital they asked if I could go and check on Elsie. Kev looked after the dogs and I went to Elsie's and found her sitting on the floor in the upstairs hall. Luckily, she'd left the front door unlocked, although I told her she mustn't do that. She'd fallen from the ladder to the small loft. Luckily, she was only on the third step when her foot slipped. But it was clear to me that she'd probably broken her ankle, and I wanted to get her checked, in case of other injuries. I called an ambulance and then collected Kev from the pub and came here because Josie had been calling you but the line was engaged and she didn't want to worry you by leaving a message.' He let out a breath as if he'd held it during his explanation.

'Is everyone still at the hospital?' Perse asked.

'As far as I know. Yes. I was going to go

with Elsie, or follow in my car but she told me it was more important that I came here to meet you. She wanted you to hear about all this in person.'

'We'll say prayers for everyone at the carol concert,' Perse said. 'If there's anything else I can do, just say the word.'

'Thanks. But they're in good hands.'

'I'd better go in then,' Perse said. 'Are you okay, Lottie? If you want me to stay with you I will.'

I was still trying to get my head around it all.

'No. You go in. People are waiting. I'm fine, thanks. And Alex and Elsie are too, so Asher says, so it's all okay.'

'They're fine. Honestly.' Asher gave me a reassuring smile. 'I wouldn't lie to you. In fact, Josie and Elsie said you, Kev and I should go ahead with our evening as planned. There's nothing any of us can do right now.'

'I'm not sure I could enjoy it knowing that all my relatives are at the hospital,' I said. 'Perhaps I should be there too?'

'But it is what they wanted. And you going to the hospital won't help. Do you really want to spend an evening in a hospital waiting room? Because that's all you'd be doing. Even Josie said that she's going to be sending Liam back with the kids so that they don't have to be there.'

'Really?'

'Yes. Really.'

'I'm happy to look after Merry,' Kev said, 'if you do want to go. But I agree with Asher. It doesn't do any good to sit around taking up space in the waiting room. And I know I only met you all today, but I don't think they'd all want you to sit there worrying. I'm sure they'll call you if there's any news.'

'You're probably right.'

I wasn't totally convinced but I didn't want to leave Merry again today unless I absolutely had to. I think she'd picked up on the fact that all was not right with the world and she was sticking to my calf as if she was attached with glue.

Twenty

Needless to say, neither the carol concert nor the Meet and Mingle Jingle were as much fun as they would've been. But even so, the carols were melodic and the organ accompaniment – on a real organ, much to my surprise, was magical.

Asher and Kev were good company and both men complemented me on my plum-coloured dress. I knew it would suit me the moment I'd seen it in the shop window, and with my strawberry-blonde hair hanging loose around my shoulders, having been washed and blow-dried into a tumble of curls at the Easterhill Spa, I was sure the admiring glances were genuine.

But knowing everyone was at the hospital took much of the shine off the evening.

After the carols, Perse announced that we should all adjourn to the hall, where the Meet and Mingle Jingle was about to start, and the church bells rang out to prove it.

I was tempted to try my hand at ringing them but I couldn't summon up the enthusiasm – until Asher and Kev made a bet as to who could do better out of the two of them. I held George's lead while Kev and Asher gave it their all. I thought Asher had possibly done it before but he promised he hadn't.

'I've been tempted,' he said, 'but I've never done it.'

I think they were trying to play Jingle Bells but as they were so out of tune and out of time, it was difficult to tell. It made everyone laugh and clap along though and after a while, even I forgot how anxious I was feeling.

I thought we'd need to go outside and enter the hall through the door I'd seen that first day I arrived, but Asher informed us there was a door to the hall from inside the church. It was hidden behind a heavy, red velvet curtain and it creaked when he opened it.

The hall was as cheerfully decorated on the inside as it was on the outside. A Christmas tree stood in one corner, it's pine-scented branches weighed down with baubles, tinsel, ribbons and lights, together with a large quantity of foil-covered, chocolate decorations and red and white striped candy canes. There were also some Christmas biscuits dangling on silver ribbons. Little fingers soon made short work of those, along with the candy canes and the chocolates.

'Good thing there are more where they came from,' Perse said, as she greeted us again with a cheerful smile. 'Between now and Christmas morning I'll have to replenish those at least once a day.'

'That's what Christmas is all about,' Kev said. 'Eating as much as possible, especially if it's something that's bad for us.'

'Is it?' Perse smiled at him. 'I thought it had something to do with the birth of Jesus, but I may be wrong.'

'Oh yeah. That too.' He winked at her and smiled.

To one side of the hall was a line of tables, covered with festive, plastic table cloths, each table piled high with plates, bowls and even buckets of food and there were also two huge punch bowls, one filled with mulled wine and one with a non-alcoholic equivalent.

The buffet was delicious. We'd stopped for lunch today and had a Christmas dinner, but I had forgotten how tiring shopping can be. The massages, manicure and pedicure, along with the complimentary head massage my hair stylist gave me were all extremely relaxing but seemed to burn calories because my tummy had started rumbling not long after Kev and Asher began to ring the bells. As soon as they had declared a draw, we had headed to the hall for food.

Strictly speaking, we should've brought

something, but I'd completely forgotten that's what we were supposed to do. Perse said it wasn't a problem and that there was always more than enough to go around.

'And if we run out,' she said, 'we can always send out an SOS to Mikkel. He's donated several delicious dishes from his restaurant but he said he was happy to provide more if needed.'

Josie called me while Asher, Kev and I were sitting at a table, stuffing our faces with hot sausage and cranberry puffs, mince pies with melt-in-the-mouth flaky pastry and so much icing sugar dusting that it fell like snow onto my dress. The Portobello mushrooms topped with candied nuts and blue cheese were heaven on a plate. I just had to get that recipe. Merry and George sat under the table, wolfing down the scraps that the three of us shared with them.

'Hi Josie,' I said, swallowing my last bite and trying not to choke. 'How're Elsie and Alex? Is everything okay? Should I come? I'm happy to.'

Josie gave a small laugh. 'No. You stay there and enjoy yourself. We're on our way and we'll be with you very soon. Diana is staying with Alex and flatly refuses to let anyone stay with them, so we're bringing the kids back too. Along with Aunt Elsie who insists that she can't miss the Meet and Mingle Jingle completely.

It's a bit cramped in this people carrier.' She laughed again.

'Save me some food,' Orla yelled. 'I'm starving.'

'Save me some mulled wine,' Elsie shouted. 'I'm gasping.'

'Save me a seat,' Josie said loudly. 'I'm shattered.'

'Save me and Toby from all these noisy women,' Liam joked.

'Ignore him,' Josie said, laughing. 'See you soon. About fifteen minutes or so, traffic permitting.'

'That was Josie,' I told Asher and Kev.

'I thought it might be.' Asher winked at me and grinned.

'They're coming here. And Elsie's coming to, so she must be okay, mustn't she?'

I was so relieved. Far more than I thought I'd be. In less than two days, I'd grown very fond of my new relatives. Especially Aunt Elsie.

'Who's that?' Kev said, as a tall, slim woman with long, jet black hair, startingly vivid green eyes and the clearest, palest skin I'd ever seen, smiled and waved.

'I have no idea,' I said.

'That's Lucy Willis.' Asher waved back. 'She's a school teacher in Easterhill. She lives in a cottage in the next road down from mine.'

Lucy must've had an excellent salary. Or a large limit on her credit card. I recognised designer labels when I saw them. Everything she wore must've had one. From the sparkling diamante hair band, the dangly, diamond earrings, the low-cut silk blouse and the bolero-style cashmere cardigan, the leather skirt and the thigh-length boots. No doubt her tights and underwear were designer, too. Assuming she was wearing any. Judging by the pert breasts and prominent nipples, her underwear was probably the finest lace.

Asher didn't seem to notice but Kev was looking at her in the same way I was looking at the plate of those stuffed mushrooms.

'Is she single?' Kev's gaze followed her as she sashayed away.

'Yep,' Asher said. 'She had a bit of a thing for Liam. But I think they only dated once. That was before he started seeing Josie.'

'Does she like dogs?'

Asher grinned. 'You're not that bad looking. Just joking. Er. I don't know. Why don't you ask her?'

'I think I might.' Kev smiled at us. 'Wish me luck. I'm not sure I could handle a second rejection in one week.'

'She'd be crazy to reject you,' I said. 'Just as crazy as your ex.'

He wasn't listening. He was already on his way towards Lucy.

Asher gave a little cough. 'You like him, don't you?'

'Yes. He's lovely. I hope she doesn't reject him. She looks a bit...'

I let my voice trail off. She was obviously a friend of Asher's and I didn't want him to think I was the sort of woman who slagged off other women, especially exceedingly beautiful and glamorous women.

'Cold? Cruel? Evil?' Asher laughed. 'I think she can be a bit of a bitch. But that's only what I've heard. And mainly from Josie and Orla. Although neither of them would lie. She was Orla's teacher last year and she really made a play for Liam but he wasn't interested. God. Listen to me. I sound like Lilith Shoe!'

He shook his head and drew his fingers across his mouth as if to zip his lips, but he was grinning.

'Lucy's not your type then?'

'Nope. What about Kev? Is he yours?'

'My type?' The question surprised me. 'I'm not sure I have a type. I just follow my heart wherever it leads me.'

He looked thoughtful. 'And how's that working out for you?'

'I think its compass may be off. It's led me in the wrong direction a few times. What about you? What's your type?'

He met my gaze and held it for a moment or two and then a slow smile crept across his lips.

'Strawberry-blonde, medium height,

expressive eyes, sensual mouth, great body, loves dogs. Know anyone like that?'

I heard myself gasp and then I choked. He handed me his glass of mulled wine as I'd finished mine, and I glugged it down, feeling the colour rise in my cheeks but hoping he'd think it was caused by my coughing.

'Thanks,' I said, handing him back the empty glass.

'Anytime. But you didn't answer my question. About Kev, I mean. Are you interested in him?'

'Kev? No. And if I were, I don't think I'd fancy my chances. Lucy has clearly taken his breath away. Which just goes to prove that his ex wasn't really The One. If she had been he wouldn't be able to forget her so quickly and move on to someone else. She did them both a favour when she rejected his proposal.'

'Or he could be putting on a brave face. If you tell a woman how you feel and she doesn't feel the same, there's not much you can do about that, except wallow in self-pity, find someone else to distract you, or open up your heart to the prospect of a new, and hopefully more promising, love.'

'You sound as if you're speaking from experience.'

Was he talking about how he felt for Josie this summer? Lilith had said he'd fallen hard.

'When you get to your late thirties and

you're single, I think it's fairly safe to say you've been through the mill a time or two. Unless you're a cold-hearted bastard who doesn't give a damn, or a loner who prefers his own company. And I don't think I'm either of those.'

The slow smile spread across his lips again and his eyes seemed to gaze into my soul.

'We're here!'

Josie's voice made me jump. Asher got to his feet, threw me an odd look, almost as if he were slightly irritated by the intrusion, and went to help Liam who was assisting Elsie inside. Everyone turned to greet Josie, Elsie, Liam and the kids, and it took me a while to make my way through the crowd around Elsie.

'Can we let Elsie sit down, please?' Josie said, smiling and tutting as she carefully created a path to the nearest chair.

'Don't fuss, honey bee,' Elsie said. 'I'm fine.'

'Are you?' I asked, finally arriving at her side.

She beamed at me as if she hadn't seen me for days. 'Oh, hello, Lottie. You look absolutely beautiful. Are you having fun? I hope my silly accident and Alex's predicament haven't ruined the day.'

I stared at her, speechless for a while. Was she seriously more concerned about me having fun than she was about her injuries? Or Alex's?

'Never mind about me. How are you?'

'Looking forward to some of the delicious food I can see over there and a drink.'

'I'll get them for you,' Josie said. 'Just remember you've got a broken ankle, will you? I'd better not come back and find you dancing with Liam.'

Elsie's laugh rang out as the rest of the merrymakers went off to enjoy themselves once more.

'Sometimes you're no fun at all,' she said.

'I'll make sure she doesn't move,' said Liam.

'How's Alex?' I asked him.

He shook his head and ran a hand through his hair as he glanced at Asher who was standing close by now that Elsie was seated.

'I don't know what happened or what the hell is going on. Even at the hospital, it didn't make much sense. The police were there asking questions. From what I can make out, it seems that some woman who Alex had been sleeping with, but had recently dumped, tried to run down Diana tonight. But Alex saved her. Luckily for Alex, the car only caught his side but he's got a broken leg, a broken arm, two fractured ribs and several lacerations, along with a mass of bruises, not to mention concussion. He'll likely be in hospital over Christmas. But the police seem to think this woman may also have been the hit and run driver who killed Bernice. Can that really be true?'

'Lilith told me earlier that she'd heard that.'

Liam, Asher and Elsie all stared at me.

'What?' Asher said. 'When was this?'

'As I was on my way here. I didn't know if it was true or just gossip, but it seems it might have been true. It was Marina. That was the name Lilith mentioned.'

Josie had returned with Elsie's food and drink.

'Marina? Is that who the police think it was? Bloody hell! That was the woman Alex recently dumped. The one Bernice advised him to if he wanted to patch things up with Di. But how could she run down Bernice and get away with it and then drive down here and try to do the same thing to Di? If the police suspected her, why hadn't they arrested her? And is the woman completely crazy?'

'She must be,' Liam said. 'Or temporarily insane. Love can drive people to do terrible things.'

'I think the police may have been about to arrest her,' I said. 'That's the impression I got from Lilith. How her friend knew is beyond me.'

Asher smiled wanly. 'Lilith and her friends know everything before anyone else. It's amazing. This Marina obviously thought she had nothing to lose. If she couldn't have Alex, then nor could Diana – was that her reasoning?'

'That should be a lesson to us all,' Elsie said. 'Be careful who you go to bed with.'

I might've been imagining it, but I'm sure Asher looked at me when Elsie said that.

'Alex will be okay though, won't he?' I asked.

'The doctors seem to think so,' Josie said. 'Right now I'm more concerned about Elsie. She flatly refuses to come and stay with us, and she can't go to Diana's until we know when Diana will be home. Becca and Toby are staying with us tonight, along with Henry, of course. Which reminds me, we must go and get him. We thought it best to leave him where he was while we were at the hospital.'

'I could've brought him with us,' Asher said.

'I know. But it was all getting so complicated. He's fine. He doesn't mind being alone for an hour or two. Unless there's a storm. Henry hates storms.'

She threw Liam an odd smile and he smiled back, that sparkle in his eyes clearly visible again.

'I'll go and get him now,' Liam said, 'and I'll take Toby and Becca to get some things.'

'Try and make sure they don't see any blood, if possible,' Josie whispered, even though they and Orla were several feet away, talking to some other teenagers.

Liam nodded, kissed her on the cheek and called over to the kids.

'So back to you, Elsie.' Josie frowned at her.

'I'll be fine, honey bee.'

Josie tutted. 'You won't be able to get upstairs without help. How, exactly, will you be fine?'

'Er. Please say no if you don't like the idea,' I said. 'But I could stay with you, Elsie. You did ask me to stay, yesterday. Unless you were just being polite.'

'I'd love that.' Elsie beamed at me. 'I know you were concerned about leaving Lilith in the lurch, but as I said yesterday, I'm happy to pay for the remainder of your booking.'

'That's fantastic,' Josie said. 'I won't have to worry about you if I know Lottie's there. Are you sure you don't mind, Lottie?'

'No. I don't mind at all. I'd love to be of help.'

'That's settled then,' said Elsie. 'Now, Asher, why don't you ask my gorgeous niece to dance?'

'Should we be dancing when Alex is in the hospital?' he queried.

'Definitely,' Elsie said. 'No matter how bad things are, there's always a reason to dance. And I meant Lottie, in case you're in any doubt.'

Asher smiled. 'I'm not in any doubt.'

And as the dulcet tones of Michael Bublé singing *White Christmas* wafted around the hall, Asher reached out his hand and I placed mine in his.

Twenty-One

It seemed strange waking up in the guest bedroom in Seaside Cottage, but when I glanced at my watch, it was only 6 a.m. and I felt as though I'd slept for twelve hours. Which of course I hadn't.

After the Meet and Mingle Jingle ended and Liam had returned with Henry and the kids, Josie and Liam took Elsie back to Seaside Cottage and took the kids home with them. Liam offered to drive me to the Sunrise B&B to collect my things but I wanted Merry to have a walk before we settled in at Aunt Elsie's, so one of Asher and Liam's friends, Jonno and Jonno's wife Sandra, said they would walk with me. They lived in The Heights, the road below Rock Road and the B&B.

Asher insisted on accompanying us because, as he said, if I was staying at Elsie's I'd be walking back down and I'd need a hand with my luggage. I pointed out that I had a car parked outside the B&B so all I'd need to do was pack my bags and toss them in the boot and then drive to Elsie's. Even so, Asher said I'd need a hand. I didn't want to argue. I rather liked the prospect of spending more time with him.

The four of us chatted non-stop and when Jonno and Sandra left us at the corner of their road, I felt as if we'd been friends for years. I'd discovered Jonno was a handyman and the one to call if anything in the village needed attention. He'd changed locks on doors after the spate of burglaries in the summer, and replaced roof tiles on the church and a couple of the shops when a storm had hit the coast in early November. He had fixed plumbing leaks, and painted ceilings, and was happy to do anything from changing a lightbulb to rewiring an entire house, or hanging a picture to building a wall. Basically it seemed, you named it, Jonno did it. He also drove a mini cab.

Sandra, who was at least ten years younger than Jonno, was petite and extremely pretty, with long curly, brown hair and the kind of face that didn't need any make-up to look good. Her voice was a soft squeak and if she had a job, she didn't mention it. I liked them both immediately.

Asher and I hardly spoke during the few minutes it took to get to the B&B; I just said how lovely I thought Jonno and Sandra were and he agreed. It was as if we had both suddenly become shy.

'I'll wait here,' Asher said, avoiding the mistletoe as he stood on the pavement, his hands stuffed into his pockets.

'Come inside. I might be a while. I need to pack and speak to Lilith.'

He glanced across the road to the house situated on the cliff opposite where several lights were blazing in the large, mullioned windows of the imposing home I'd admired when I'd first spotted it.

'Actually,' he said, pointing towards the house. 'I'm just going to nip over and see if Mikkel's home. He wasn't in the pub earlier and I haven't seen him since he and Diana broke up yesterday. Why don't you text me when you're done, and I'll be back?'

'Okay.'

So that was Mikkel's house. Wow. He was clearly rich. But then he did own a pub, a restaurant and a nightclub, not forgetting The Boathouse.

That made me smile. I thought of Kev and how he was dancing with Lucy for most of the night and was about to walk her home when we all left. She hadn't rejected him and from what I'd seen, they seemed to be hitting it off. I wouldn't be at all surprised if Kev had more than George and all of us for company this Christmas. Although when I mentioned it to Josie, she turned up her nose and shrugged.

Lucy clearly wasn't Josie's favourite person. Was that because Lucy had had a crush on Liam? Or was there more to that story than I'd heard?

It hadn't taken me long to pack and Lilith was both understanding and eager to hear the entire story when I told her where I was going and briefly what had happened. I didn't want to gossip but felt I owed her that much at least. Besides, she'd find out soon enough whether or not I told her.

'I hope they catch her,' was all Lilith said, which surprised me. And then she added, 'and preferably before the crazy woman goes to the hospital, or to Diana's home when no one's there to protect her, and tries again.'

I hadn't thought of that and although I didn't think that would happen, I called Josie and mentioned it.

'I hadn't thought of that,' Josie said. 'I'll call Diana now and make sure the police are nearby, just in case. I can't believe Marina would really try again, but then I can't believe anyone would be crazy enough to try to run over another person on purpose, so anything's possible. I'll also insist Diana comes and stays with us until Marina's apprehended.'

'I think that's probably a good idea,' I said.

It was gone 10 by the time I texted Asher and he was back at my car five minutes later.

'How's Mikkel?' I asked.

'Better than I expected. He said he wasn't that surprised Diana had given Alex another chance. He just hoped Alex didn't blow it and let her and the kids down. That's typical of Mikkel. Always thinking of others. It'll take him a while to get over her, I think, but he's definitely not weeping and wailing or even feeling sorry for himself, so that's a good thing. How was Lilith?'

I smiled. 'Ditto.'

He carried my bags to the car while I made sure I kept a tight hold on Merry's lead.

'Would you like me to drive?' he offered. 'The roads are pretty icy even though the gritters have been out.'

I raised my brows in mock consternation.

'Are you offering because I'm a woman and you don't think women can cope with icy roads? Or is it because you think I might be a bad driver?'

He looked genuinely contrite.

'I apologise. That did sound somewhat condescending. What I meant was that some people don't like driving in snow and ice. I might've offered even if you'd been a man.'

I grinned at him. That was actually very thoughtful. And rather sweet.

'In that case, thanks. I've just realised that I'm probably over the limit, so unless you're over the limit too, that might not be a bad idea. We had a couple of glasses of wine with lunch, and bubbly at the Easterhill Spa, plus I had one or two glasses of mulled wine at the Meet and Mingle Jingle.'

Our shopping trip and pampering session seemed a long time ago now after everything that had happened.

'It sounds as if you had a lovely day.' He grinned before becoming serious. 'Until this evening, that is, when things went pear-shaped with Alex, Diana and Elsie. I only had two halves of lager in the pub with Kev, and one glass of mulled wine, which was more than enough for me, so I should be fine to drive.'

'Not a lover of mulled wine?'

'Let's just say it's not my drink of choice.'

He didn't mention that I drank half of his mulled wine, when he offered it to me while I was choking ... after he had made it perfectly clear that I was his type and he was interested in me.

Which I still couldn't quite believe.

Coming to Seahorse Harbour was without doubt the best decision I had made in years.

Asher was a good driver and we were at Elsie's a few minutes later. He even managed to get up the drive without skidding at all on the ice. I'm not sure I could've done that, but I didn't tell him so.

I'd apologised when I realised he would have to walk home from Elsie's, instead of me dropping him at his cottage on the way, as I'd intended. But he told me not to give that a second thought.

'I could use some more fresh air and it's only a couple of minutes' walk from here.'

He carried my bags inside but declined the offer of a glass of Elsie's egg-nog.

'It's Monday tomorrow and I need a clear head for my surgery. I also need to make sure my place is spotless for when my parents and sister arrive, so I don't need a headache, thanks.'

'My egg-nog won't give you a headache,' Elsie said.

'It did last year.'

'Ah. But you had more than one glass, I seem to recall.'

'Yes. And that's the problem. It's so delicious that I'll want more than one.'

He smiled good-naturedly and to my surprise, he bent down and kissed Elsie on the cheek. She was sitting on the sofa nearest to the fire with her foot resting on a padded footstool.

'And if I were Lottie's age, I'd want more than one of those kisses,' she said, her eyes dancing with mischief. 'Although not on my cheek.'

He grinned and shot a look at me and I could feel the heat rise to my cheeks.

'I'll walk you to the door.' I turned away so that he couldn't see my blushes.

'I get the distinct impression Elsie's

playing matchmaker,' he said, grinning even more as I opened the front door.

'Yes. Er. Sorry about that.'

Our eyes met briefly until I looked away.

'No need to apologise as far as I'm concerned.'

'Oh. Okay. Er. Thanks for everything tonight,' I said, not really sure how to respond to that in case I said something stupid. 'In spite of what happened with Alex and Elsie, I had a lovely time.'

'Me too.'

He hesitated at the door and I cursed the fact that Elsie hadn't put up any mistletoe. I'd have to have a word with her about that.

'Good night then,' I said. 'Pleasant dreams.'

'They will be. I hope yours will be too. Good night, gorgeous.'

Merry barked and I realised that, once again, Asher was calling my dog gorgeous, not me. I wasn't aware that she'd followed us to the front door until that moment.

'See you soon, I hope,' I said.

'Definitely.' He looked into my eyes and held my gaze. 'I think it's pretty obvious I like you, Lottie.'

'You do?'

'Why the surprise? Haven't I made that clear?'

'I ... Er ... I wasn't sure.'

'I'll make it clear now then. Unless you don't feel the same about me. But I think I'm on safe ground. I've seen it in your eyes.'

There was no point in denying it.

'I do like you. I like you a lot. It's a pity there's no mistletoe.'

He beamed at me.

'I feel the same about you.' He stepped closer. 'And who needs mistletoe?'

He took me in his arms and eased me towards his body. Mine tingled with excitement and expectation but he didn't kiss me straight away and as I looked into his eyes, I worried he might be having second thoughts.

A slow smile spread across his gorgeous mouth and as if he could read my mind he said, 'I was waiting for you to say something. The last time I kissed you, you had a few things to say beforehand.'

'I was nervous.'

'So was I. You're not nervous now?'

I slowly shook my head. 'Not nervous, no. This time I'm excited. That was a really good kiss.'

'It was. But I have an inkling that this one will be even better.'

And he was right. It was.

Either someone was ringing the bells of St Mary Star of the Sea, or I was falling in love with Asher Bryant.

Twenty-Two

Elsie and I stayed up and chatted for at least an hour.

We talked about Asher, and Elsie confirmed that she was hoping we would get together.

'Asher's one of the good ones, sweetheart. From what you've told me, you haven't had a lot of men like that in your life as far as romance is concerned.'

'You're right. I haven't. But I'm only here for a week. It would be lovely to have a holiday fling with Asher, but the problem is, I think I may already have feelings for him and that's probably not a good thing.'

'Why not? I think it's wonderful. And it doesn't have to be just a week, does it? You said yourself that you're only renting where you live, and you no longer have a job or any other reason to keep you in Reading. Would it be so bad to spend more time in Seahorse Harbour? Or maybe even move here permanently?'

Elsie was saying all the things I'd been thinking.

'It wouldn't be bad at all. I think it would be the perfect place to live, especially because it would mean I could spend more time with you and Josie and Diana. But what if things didn't work out with me and Asher? Or what if he's only interested in having a holiday romance with me in the full knowledge that I'll be going back to Reading? He was seeing Josie in the summer, knowing that she might be returning to New York. Perhaps he's not looking for a serious relationship.'

'Perhaps he simply hasn't found the right one. Until now. I've seen the way he looks at you and believe me, I've never seen him look at anyone quite like that. Not even Josie. Yes. He was quite keen on her, but I think that was more because Josie is a force of nature. She can sweep you up into her life before you realise it. And I mean that in a good way.'

'She's your favourite, isn't she? There's a real bond between the two of you.'

Elsie looked a little flustered but her smile was full of love.

'I'll admit I do have a slight preference for spending time with Josie rather than with Diana. But I wouldn't say either of them was my favourite. That position is reserved for someone else.'

She didn't elaborate and as I had no idea

who that could be, I didn't feel I should ask. Perhaps she meant the man Josie had told me Elsie was seeing in the summer. Mikkel's dad. I think his name was Gray.

She suddenly changed the subject and we talked about Diana and Alex, and Marina and Alex's affair. She told me of his others and she filled me in on Bernice.

She also told me the history between Alex and Josie, and I was astonished to hear that they were once deeply in love. Josie had told me a bit about everyone's past but she'd skimmed over that part. But I was more amazed to hear how Diana had behaved and the dreadful thing she'd done to make sure they broke up. How could Diana do that to her sister?

Elsie went on to tell me about Josie and Liam and the part Lucy had played in trying to make sure they didn't become a couple. That made me a bit anxious for Kev and I decided I'd have to ensure he was okay the following day.

By the time I helped Elsie upstairs to bed, it was 1 a.m. and I now understood a lot more about many of the people I cared about in Seahorse Harbour.

But I still didn't know that much about Aunt Elsie.

Twenty-Three

I was pleased to find that the cottage was warm when I awoke on Monday morning, but not as stiflingly hot as my room in the B&B.

I went downstairs to make coffee with the intention of taking Elsie a cup and checking she was okay and didn't need anything before I took Merry out for a quick pee prior to having a shower and getting dressed. But when I drew back the curtains in the kitchen and unlocked the door with the key from the rack beside it, I got the shock of my life. There was a full-on blizzard outside and I couldn't see past the terrace in the garden.

Actually, blizzard wasn't the right word for it. There wasn't any wind.

White-out was a better description.

I'd read that on one of Clark's social media updates a few days before. He'd said there had been a white-out and as they couldn't see beyond their outstretched hands, he and his friends, including the blonde woman, whose

219

name was Samantha, had spent the entire day in the chalet, making use of its many facilities, such as the sauna, the hot tub on the decking outside, and the cosy TV room.

I didn't need to be a genius to know that Clark and Samantha had probably had sex in each one of those places.

But I realised now, I didn't care. I also realised I hadn't checked his updates since meeting Asher. Clark was history, so that was another good thing about coming to Seahorse Harbour.

This white-out wasn't good though and Merry looked at me as if to say, 'Seriously? You expect me to go out and pee in that?'

But she clearly needed to so she sniffed and inched and bounced her way across the snow-covered terrace. Her long ears flapped up and down like the wings of a bird struggling to take flight, and most of her body disappeared beneath several inches of snow.

She didn't stay out long and when she raced back in, her paws skidding on the floor, I quickly closed the door behind her to keep out the curtain of snow.

I immediately thought of Diana. If she was still at the hospital, she wouldn't be able to make it home in this.

I dried Merry's fur with kitchen towel and she slumped in front of the radiator while I made some coffee and then followed me back upstairs as I took a cup up for Elsie together with one for me.

I softly tapped on Elsie's half-open door. She'd asked me to leave it that way last night. Or I should say, earlier that morning.

'Come in,' she called out, cheerily.

'Good morning,' I said. 'How are you feeling today? You'll never believe the weather. I hope you don't mind but I think Merry peed on your terrace.'

'Good morning, sweetheart,' she said, and the way she said it reminded me of Mum, but I didn't know why. 'I feel fine, thank you. Rain or snow? I do hope it's snow. It would be lovely to have a white Christmas. And please don't worry about the terrace. Merry is welcome to pee anywhere ... within reason.'

'I don't know about a white Christmas. It's definitely a white-out, out there. I couldn't even see your garden.' I put her coffee on the bedside table, along with milk and sugar. 'I didn't know how you liked it. Shall I draw your curtains and then you can see the weather for yourself, although it is still dark out there.'

'Yes please. And thank you for the coffee. Milk, no sugar, for future reference.'

I added the milk to Elsie's coffee and she smiled as I went to the windows and drew back the curtains.

'Ta dah!'

'Gosh. You weren't joking. I hope Diana

came home last night because she'll never get back in this. How deep is the snow?'

'Merry disappeared beneath it and she had to bounce her way outside, so several inches, I would say.'

Elsie flipped back the duvet and patted the empty space beside her.

'Come and get in with me and we'll all snuggle up and watch it together, including you, Merry.'

Mum and I often did that and although I hadn't known Elsie for long, it didn't seem at all strange that she'd suggest it. It seemed the most natural thing in the world and I loved the fact that she was happy for Merry to cuddle up on her bed.

She propped up the pillows and I got in beside her. Merry jumped up and lay between us, stretched out fully and enjoying the tummy rub that Elsie was giving her.

I wasn't sure how long we sat there, chatting and laughing and watching the morning light try to pierce its way through the curtain of white, but by the time I eventually got showered and dressed it was almost 9 a.m. and still snowing heavily.

I helped Elsie to the shower in her room and was glad to see there was a built-in rail she could hang onto and even a drop-down stool, so she didn't need me to help her.

'I had them fitted for the future,' Elsie said.

'To avoid unnecessary drilling and damage to the tiles at a later date. The only way I'll be leaving this place is in a box.'

I wished she hadn't said that and she must've read my mind because she added, 'And that won't be for at least another twenty years or more.'

I helped her down the stairs because she refused to spend the day in bed even though Josie had told me that the doctor said Elsie should rest and keep her foot raised.

'Only old or sick people spend the day in bed,' she said. 'Or lovers. I'm not old or sick and sadly, I don't have anyone around at the moment, who falls into the last category.'

'Do you wish you'd married again?'

'Good God no! Sorry. That sounded as though my marriage was awful, and it wasn't. It was wonderful. Eric was a truly good man. But I'm simply not cut out to be a wife. And I love my own company. Plus I have lovely family and friends and neighbours so I'm never lonely. That's one of the good things about living in a place like Seahorse Harbour. Everyone knows everyone else. Of course that does also have a downside, as poor Mikkel will be finding out right now. Everyone knows your business and they'll all offer help and advice.'

'Do you...?' I wasn't sure I should ask.

'Do I what, sweetheart?'

I sat her on the sofa where she'd been last

night and began to make the fire which she'd shown me how to bank up before we'd gone to bed.

'Do you ever wish you'd had children?'

She made a strange sound but when I looked at her, her eyes were cast to one side as if she were looking back into the past or something and she didn't answer for a while. I was about to apologise in case I'd upset her, when she let out a long sigh and smiled.

'Sometimes I wish I'd been different. I wish I'd been the type of woman who really wanted a family of her own. But it simply wasn't me. I'm not sure I'd have made a good mother. I think I might've followed in my own mum's footsteps and I never wanted that. People seem to think they all have a right to be parents, however ill-suited they are to the job. And it is a job to bring up a child. It's a full-time occupation. Not everyone thinks they're able to be an astronaut, or a politician, or a bus driver, or a builder, but everyone thinks they'll be the perfect parent. That it'll all come naturally. But it doesn't. Some people are lousy parents. Some people shouldn't have children. I was sure I was one of those people. And I'm positive I made the right decision.'

'I must admit, sometimes I wonder if I'm cut out for motherhood. I discussed it with Mum a few times. She and Dad were definitely born to be parents. They were perfect and I had the happiest childhood anyone could hope for. But when I think of my future, it doesn't necessarily include a child. I thought a husband and a family was what I wanted, but a part of me was never completely sure. Mum said that I shouldn't worry about it. That it was perfectly okay not to want a child. What was important was to love the people who came into my life and to do the best I could for them.'

'Your mum was a very clever woman.'

'Yes. She was. I still miss her dreadfully.'

'Of course you do. And you will always miss her. It's right that we should miss the ones we love. But that doesn't mean we should mourn them forever, or put our lives on hold, or wallow in grief. I'm not suggesting you're doing any of those things because you're not. All I'm saying is that we don't have to be miserable after we lose a loved one. And they wouldn't want us to be. We should find a way to celebrate their lives and to find joy in something every day.'

'Please don't take this the wrong way, but that's why I couldn't come and stay with you sooner. You always seemed so full of life and after Mum and Dad died, I think I did want to shut myself away. I definitely did wallow, I'll admit that, and I made a lot of silly decisions. I was grieving and I didn't want to be around people who weren't.'

'But you got through it, sweetheart. And

you're here now.'

'I'm frightened I may still be making silly decisions though. Clark and that job were bad decisions. Now I don't have either. Coming here was a spur-of-the moment decision. And that's one thing that I did get right, I think. But where do I go from here? I think ... No. I know I'm falling for Asher, and yet I hardly know him. I didn't admit this last night when we were chatting, but I even considered moving here after only being here for a day. How crazy is that?'

She reached out and stroked my cheek while Merry nuzzled her way in front of me so that she could sprawl out before the fire I'd just lit.

'That's not crazy at all. Sometimes we just know where we're meant to be. And you could do far worse than fall for Asher, as I told you. He's a wonderful man. I can assure you moving here is one of the best things I ever did. But if you don't mind me giving you a piece of advice it's this: Don't be in a hurry to plan your future. Relax and enjoy the moment and let life sort out the rest. It often does, you know. I'm not saying you shouldn't chase your dreams. Of course you should. You can't just sit back and expect them to sort themselves out and come to you. But sometimes, if we don't have dreams, or plans, or schemes, and we just go with the flow, life leads us to where we should be. And I have a feeling that you should be here.'

'Lilith said the seahorses called Asher here. She said they call people who they want to help them. That sounds ridiculous and yet it sounds so magical. I'm hoping perhaps, the seahorses have called me. But I have no idea how I can help them or why they'd want me, so that's probably just wishful thinking.'

'Perhaps. But some people around here do say that the seahorses have magical powers. They don't just bring people here to help them. They bring people here to make the village a better place. You'd definitely make this village a better place. At least for me. And for one or two others, I suspect. You've already made it a better place for that man, Kev who was dumped by his girlfriend. And, I think for Lucy, who was feeling very low and even considering leaving. Now I'm no matchmaker but since Lucy moved to this village, I've never seen her look so happy or relaxed as she did with Kev last night. And if you hadn't invited him to the Meet and Mingle Jingle and included him in your new-found circle, that might not have happened.'

I liked the thought of that. And of having a new-found circle.

'But he might've seen the poster for it and gone anyway. I'm not sure that's all down to me.'

'Isn't it? He was feeling miserable and thinking of going home, so he told Liam and

Asher, until he met you on the beach.'

Elsie's landline phone interrupted the conversation and when she picked it up, she smiled.

'Good morning, honey bee. Yes, yes. We're fine. And yes, we've seen the weather. No. There's no need for you to come and see me. I'm in good hands.' Elsie rolled her eyes and grinned at me, placing a hand over the mouthpiece. 'Josie's such a dear. I bet she'll be marching through the door within the next two hours.'

Elsie and Josie continued their conversation and Elsie asked about Diana and then Josie asked to speak to me.

'Good morning,' she said. 'How was last night? Did you manage okay? Is there anything you need?'

'Good morning, Josie. We're fine thanks. And no. There's nothing either of us need. How's Diana? Any news of Alex? Or of Marina?'

'Di's fine. Well ... as fine as can be expected. She came to us last night around 11 and she stayed with us. Alex was about the same and the police saw her just as she was leaving. They've caught Marina and she's been remanded in custody or something so there's no need to worry on that score anymore, thank heavens. It's terrible weather but I'll pop around later, just to say hello. Let me know if you do decide you need anything.'

I promised her I would and we said goodbye but sure enough, a little under two hours later, Josie arrived at the front door.

Twenty-Four

'What were you going into the loft for anyway?' Josie asked, as we sat around the fire drinking hot chocolate and eating mince pies.

We'd been discussing the events of yesterday and how Elsie falling just moments after Alex and Diana's brush with near-death at the hands of Marina was a spooky coincidence.

'What? Oh nothing. Nothing at all.'

Elsie seemed flustered.

Josie tutted. 'You must've wanted something otherwise you wouldn't have tried to go up there. But why didn't you just access the loft from that door in your bedroom?'

Elsie had had the attic converted into a master bedroom and en suite but there was still a small trap hatch to a part of the loft situated in the upstairs hall. It was at the same end as the flight of stairs to Elsie's bedroom.

'Because I must've pushed one of the trunks up against the door by mistake. I couldn't budge the door from my room.'

'Right. Lottie and I will go and sort that out right now.'

Josie got up and nodded her head towards the hall. I got up and followed her. Merry made a small bark but when I told her to stay, she let her head flop back down onto the rug, sighing contentedly.

'No,' Elsie said. 'There's really no need. It can wait.'

'Tell us what you wanted and we'll bring it down.'

Josie was clearly determined.

'Er. I wanted some more decorations. I'm sure there's another box up there and if there is it'll be this end of the loft, not at the other end, so if it's not there, don't worry.'

Josie laughed as we pulled down the ladder and climbed into the loft.

'Anyone would think she doesn't want us up here. I wonder what she's hiding.'

I didn't think we should try to find out but I did agree that Elsie seemed anxious. As soon as we got up there, we heard her calling from downstairs, although we could only just make out what she was saying.

'It's dirty and dusty up there. Honestly, just forget it. I don't need any more decorations.'

Josie grinned. 'She's definitely got something up here she doesn't want us to see.'

Josie glanced around as she switched on

the light, illuminating piles of cardboard boxes stacked high and several wooden trunks. All the boxes had what was inside, written on the fronts and tops as did most of the trunks. None of them had the words, 'Christmas decorations' written on them.

'Let's move those two trunks away from the door,' Josie said. 'At least then Elsie can get in her from her bedroom, once her ankle has healed, that is.'

We moved some cardboard boxes and the first trunk which was extremely heavy. No wonder Elsie couldn't get the door to budge. The second trunk behind the first looked completely different to anything else up there. It was painted white and had large pink hearts painted all over it. It was the sort of thing you'd expect to see in a girl's bedroom as something to hold her toys or personal belongings. I wondered if it had been Elsie's when she was a child, but it didn't look quite that old although it was definitely not new.

'This one's different,' Josie said, grinning at me. 'I wonder what's in here.'

'We can't look,' I said. 'It might contain confidential papers or things that Elsie wouldn't want us to see.'

'Which is exactly why I need to take a peek. Don't look at me like that. Elsie won't mind.'

'You said yourself you thought there was something she didn't want us to see. Perhaps this is it. We mustn't look. Not without her permission. It's not right.'

Josie looked torn but in the end she shrugged.

'Okay. Let's just move it away from the door. I'll ask her about when we go back down.'

We'd expected it to be as heavy as the last one so we both gripped it tight but it was much lighter and as we shifted it over with all our might, the lid flipped open.

Josie glanced at me and grinned.

'We didn't open it. It opened itself.'

I knew I shouldn't but I couldn't help myself. It was as if something inside the trunk was calling to me. But that's probably just the excuse I used to take a peek.

The trunk was piled high with envelopes.

'Oh look!' Josie said, excitement in her voice. 'Do you think these are love letters?' She reached in and grabbed a handful.

I recognised the writing immediately. It was Mum's handwriting. Mum had obviously written to Aunt Elsie a great deal over the years. But why had Elsie kept the letters?

'No,' I snapped. 'That's my mum's handwriting.'

Josie gave me the strangest look and leant towards me, the letters still held firmly in her grasp.

'Your mum's handwriting? Er. You don't think...?'

Her voice trailed off but I knew what she was implying.

'No I don't! Absolutely not.'

I knew, because for one very brief moment the same thought had popped into my head. But just because a woman wrote hundreds and hundreds of letters to another woman and that other woman kept them in a trunk with massive pink hearts emblazoned over it, it didn't mean they shared a secret love or anything. It just meant they were friends and they liked each other. Didn't it?

'You're right,' Josie said, grinning. 'Elsie wouldn't hide it if she loved someone. Unless the other person wanted her to.'

'No,' I said again, even more emphatically this time. 'Mum and Dad were madly, deeply and blissfully in love until the day they died.'

But Mum was always telling me how wonderful Elsie was. How loving and caring and reliable. How Elsie would always be there for me and how she loved us all deeply but she just wasn't good at relationships. But then Dad often said the same about Elsie, so that didn't mean anything. There was only one way to find out.

I took one of the letters still in the trunk – one that was clearly several years old judging by the tattered envelope and the faded ink, and opened it.

'I thought you said we shouldn't look?'

Josie reminded me, grinning.

'But that was before I saw Mum's handwriting.'

"Dearest Elsie," I read. "We're all well here, and Charlotte grows more beautiful each day."

'Oh,' I said to Josie, feeling a little relieved. 'Mum's writing to Elsie about me. She's telling her I'm growing more beautiful each day. A typical 'Mum' letter.'

I smiled and then continued to read the letter, this time, out loud.

"Words will never be enough to say how much she means to us. Or how much you mean. But we know that you're well aware of how we feel, and you've asked us not to dwell on that, so we won't. Except to say yet another massive thank you from the bottom of our hearts. All hope was lost, until you gave us the greatest gift of all. We will love you forever and beyond."

I stopped for a second. I wasn't sure where this was going but I had an uneasy feeling.

'Go on,' Josie said, her brows furrowing slightly as if she too, knew that something was about to be divulged.

I hesitated but decided to continue:

"But let us tell you more about Charlotte. She took her first, independent steps today. She's been taking a few steps for a while now, as we told you, holding our fingers in her tiny hands, but today she got up and walked from one spot to another without any help from us.

235

We were carrying her presents to her and she was sitting on the floor and when she saw us, she got up and walked towards us. The smile on her face reminded us both so much of you. Even at this age, the resemblance is evident. I can see my darling brother in her eyes. She has his hair too, but she definitely has your smile."

'What?' Josie said it at the same time I did and we stared at one another.

'Why would your mum say you have Aunt Elsie's smile? And your uncle Eric's eyes and hair?'

'Perhaps she just meant there's a strong family resemblance?'

'To your uncle Eric, maybe. But as you've said yourself, more than once, Aunt Elsie isn't a blood relative so you couldn't look like her. You couldn't have her smile.'

'I think Mum must have simply meant we have similar smiles.'

Josie nodded. 'Yes. That must be it. Read on and see what else she says.'

I didn't want to. My heart rate had suddenly increased and goosebumps were prickling my skin. I had such an uneasy feeling about this letter. But I knew I had to read it.

"We can't believe she's one, today. The last 365 days have brought us so much happiness and laughter. Sometimes it feels as if our hearts will burst. I can still remember the day she was born and I held her in my arms at the hospital, as if it were just yesterday. Sometimes I still feel that this is all just a wonderful dream and that I'll wake up from it, childless and barren as I was until that day. But I know you don't want me to say such things, so I apologise for that. I just need you to know that we will be so, so grateful to you until the day we die. And I promise you that Charlotte will have the happiest life possible. We're enclosing some more photos so that you can see for yourself how gorgeous she is. We love you so much, Elsie, and we want you to know that Charlotte will always love you too. We'll both make sure of that."

'Childless and barren?' Josie repeated the words. 'Your ... your mum was childless and barren? Then how could she have had you?'

Twenty-Five

Sometimes things are staring you in the face and yet you just can't see them.

Sometimes all the clues and evidence point you in one direction but you look the other way.

And sometimes people you love keep secrets from you, and when you discover the truth, it breaks your heart in two.

With the letter still clasped in my hand, I stumbled to the ladder and scrambled down, Josie calling my name as she hurried after me.

I couldn't think. I couldn't see clearly but I made it to the ground and then raced downstairs and into the sitting room with Josie right behind me.

Elsie looked at me with a mixture of sadness, contrition and ... love. Yes, love.

I held the crumpled letter out to her as I stood in the doorway, shaking.

'Is this true? Does it really mean what I think it does? Are you ... are you my mother?'

Elsie held my gaze for a second and then

nodded.

'Yes, Lottie. I am. I gave birth to you and Eric was your father.'

'What?' Josie shrieked. 'Lottie's your daughter? Yours and your dead husband's?'

'Yes, honey bee. She is.'

'I don't believe this,' Josie said, while I fought for words to come. 'How? Why? And that means ... oh my God, Elsie. That means you gave her up!'

'No!' Elsie tried to get to her feet but she stumbled and had to sit back down. 'I didn't give you up, Lottie. I gave you to two wonderful people who couldn't have a child of their own and desperately wanted to be parents.'

'You gave me up,' I said.

'No!' Elsie repeated. 'Let me try to explain. Please sit down so that we can talk about this.'

I shook my head. 'I can't believe Mum and Dad lied to me all these years. I can't believe I didn't find anything about my adoption. I can't believe you could do this to me, or that they could. I can't believe my entire life has been a lie.'

'Stop that!'

Elsie sounded cross but surely I was the one who had a right to feel angry?

'Were you ever going to tell me? Were they? Did they pay for me?'

'Absolutely not! How could you even think such a thing? Money didn't come into it. And I don't know if they would've told you. One day they might have. But I didn't intend to while they were alive and although I did consider it after they died, what good would it have done?'

'What good? I'd have known the truth. All these years I've believed I was their daughter, that I took after them and yet I've always wondered why we were so different in many ways. And now I know why. Because I wasn't theirs. I had no connection to them whatsoever.'

'That's not true. Lydia was Eric's sister. Eric connected you to them.'

'Was he alive? Did he agree to give me up?'

She shook her head and I remembered Mum ... well, the woman I thought was my mum, telling me that Uncle Eric died shortly before I was born.

Except he wasn't my uncle. He was my dad. And Elsie didn't really love him. She'd told me that herself. She'd said she didn't love him as much as a wife probably should love her husband. Is that why she'd given me up? She didn't want his child?

'No. Eric died before I discovered I was pregnant and although I told you I only married him to escape my mother, I loved him very much. I was devastated when he died so unexpectedly. And then I realised I was going to have a child. I couldn't bring up a child on my own. Call me a coward or whatever you like but I knew I couldn't do it. I wasn't cut out for motherhood. I never wanted children. That may sound cold and indifferent to you, but believe me that was the complete opposite of how I felt. I wanted you to have the very best life you could. And I knew that wouldn't be with me. But I knew how much Lydia wanted a child. She'd had three miscarriages and one still birth. She was Eric's sister and she and Russell were the loveliest people I'd ever known. I knew immediately what I was going to do, and when I told them, believe me, they were over the moon.'

'But Mum's never mentioned it,' Josie said, as if she was astonished by that fact.

'Your mother doesn't know. As soon as I discovered it, I told her and your dad and my own parents that I needed to get away to get over Eric's death. No one questioned that. I went away for seven months and when I returned, no one was any the wiser. We told everyone that Lydia was pregnant as soon as we'd agreed what to do, so everyone thought Lottie was hers and Russell's. She wore increasingly larger cushions beneath her clothes as the pregnancy continued. I gave birth in a private clinic and the adoption was done through a specialist firm. No one, apart from the three of us and the doctors and nurses at the clinic knew our secret.'

'And that was it? You just decided you

didn't want me and you handed me over to them?'

'No. I wanted you very much because you were a part of Eric. And I wanted you to have the best life you possibly could. That life was with Lydia and Russell, not with me. I didn't want to do to you what my mum had done to Tibby and me, and what Tibby did to Diana and Josie. I wanted you to be happy and carefree and adored and blessed and cherished. And you were, Lottie. You know you were. And not just by your parents, but also by me. I loved you then and I love you now. I just couldn't raise you as my child. I'm sorry if this hurts you now but I did what I knew was best for you. We all did. And your parents couldn't have loved you more if you were their own flesh and blood. And you were Lydia's, through Eric. So I won't apologise for what we did. It was the right thing to do. But I will apologise for hurting you now because I can see that you are hurting and if I could do anything to stop that, I would, believe me.'

'I ... I can't be here,' I said, turning towards the door and calling Merry to me.

'You can't go out in this weather!' Elsie sounded scared. 'Sweetheart, please! Don't go.'

Josie shook her head at me. 'I can understand you're devastated. I'd feel the same. I do feel the same, but obviously it's far more intense for you. But it's a white-out outside, Lottie. You can't drive anywhere in this.'

'I ... I need to get out of here and think.'

'Fine. Go to my house. Or to the Seahorse Bites Café or somewhere within a short walk from here. But leave Merry. Don't drag her out in this weather. She'll be safe and sound and here when you've had time to think this through and you can come and get her once you've done that.'

'Unless Elsie decides to give her away,' I said, rather acidly.

But I knew Josie was right and the minute I told Merry to go and sit by the fire, she dashed back to the rug.

'Lottie?' Elsie said.

'Please don't say another word.'

I turned, grabbed my coat from the stand and shoved on my boots. Josie walked to the door with me.

'We'll all be here when you come back,' she said. 'Please stay safe, and let us know where you are. I can't bear the thought of having to worry about you as well as Diana and Alex. And Elsie, too. Although at the moment, I think we could both happily strangle her.'

Twenty-Six

'Hello! What on earth are you doing out in this weather? Is everything okay?'

Asher opened the door for me and stepped aside to let me in. I'd called to his surgery, as it was Monday but there was no one there but him.

'I'm so sorry to turn up like this, especially as you're working but I didn't know where else to go and I needed a friend right now. We are friends, aren't we?'

'Yes. Of course we are. And as you can see, I'm not rushed off my feet. Only dire emergencies will make it here today. My veterinary nurse couldn't make it in. The roads are impassable and people are being advised not to ... but that doesn't matter. What's wrong, Lottie? Oh God. Has something happened to Elsie? Or to Diana, or Alex?'

I shook my head but now that I was standing in front of him, I didn't know why I was there. I had no right to burden him with my problems.

'Let's go into the sitting room. I can hear the bell if anyone wants a vet. I'll make us some coffee. Unless you'd like something stronger. You look so pale and upset. Please tell me what's wrong before I go out of my mind with worry.'

'It is Elsie. But not in the way you think. She's fine. Josie's there. And yes, please. I'd like something stronger than coffee, if you have it.'

'Brandy?'

I nodded and he led me to the sitting room with an arm wrapped around my shoulders.

Even in my misery and confusion, I couldn't help but admire his taste. His cottage was a little smaller than Elsie's but it was modern, shiny and stylish. I caught a glimpse of the kitchen which was sleek and black with red tiles. The dark green walls and black leather furniture in the sitting room should've made the room seem smaller and darker, but instead it felt warm and bright and welcoming. There was an ultra-modern and uber-stylish raised fire on one wall and the ebony wood coffee table bore a large hurricane lamp filled with black and green Christmas baubles and bright, warm white fairy lights. A surprising addition for a man like Asher.

But what surprised me most was the fact that the place was pristine. Clark's home always looked like a bomb had dropped on it.

Even the presents beneath the real Christmas tree, which was hung with red and gold baubles and adorned with a mass of warm white lights, were stacked in neat piles.

This might seem crazy, given my recent discovery, but all I could think about as I sat down on the sofa nearest the fire was that this wasn't a home for a dog.

Asher handed me a large glass of brandy and then he sat opposite and took my free hand in his.

'So tell me then. What's happened?'

I knocked back the contents of my glass and looked him in the eye.

'I don't know where to begin.'

But it all came pouring out of me. The trunk in the loft. The letters. The fact that Elsie was my biological mother. All of it. And when I'd finished, he stared at me in silent disbelief, my hand still in his, providing me some comfort and reassurance.

'I don't know what to say,' he finally managed.

'That's the problem, isn't it? What can be said? It's done. It happened. Nothing will ever change it. I'm not who I thought I was.'

'That's not entirely true. Don't glower at me like that, Lottie. You're still the same woman you were last night. You still look the same and talk the same. None of that has changed. You had two people in your life who adored you. That hasn't changed. You have one person who clearly loved you very much, and still does. That hasn't changed.'

'I don't think she loves me very much, if you mean Elsie.'

'I think she does, Lottie. I know you think Elsie gave you up, but I can see it from her side too. As she said, she didn't give you up. She gave you the best life she could. Your parents kept in constant contact with her and she kept those letters and treasured them. You don't do that unless you love someone. We can't make people who we want them to be, Lottie. Would you rather Elsie had kept you with her? Perhaps you would've both been miserable. And she said Lydia and Russell desperately wanted a child. Can't you see what a wonderful thing Elsie did for them?'

'Yes. But I was her child. Not theirs. I'm not a puppy or a toy or something. I'm a human being.'

'And one who has had a very happy life with a loving family. And who now has the chance to have another family. Perhaps not the one she expected, but family all the same. Are you going to walk away because someone did what they thought was right for everyone at the time? Are you going to punish people for showering you with love?'

'They lied to me! They all lied! Are you saying that's okay?'

He shook his head. 'No. I think they should've told you. But again, if you see it from their side, perhaps they were terrified of this. This very thing happening. Of you blaming them and hating them and turning your back on them.'

'I ... I'm not doing that. But I'm hurt. I'm confused. I'm upset.'

'And I can see all that in your eyes. You have the most expressive eyes I've ever seen.'

'Mum always said that. The woman I thought was my mum.'

'She was your mum to all intents and purposes, Lottie.'

'And I loved her so much and now I find out she'd lied to me every single day.'

'No. She kept the truth from you. Truth sometimes hurts and it's not always better to know it. She did what she thought was best for you and for her and her husband. And for Elsie too. You don't feel better for knowing the truth, do you? And be honest here. Who was being hurt by you not knowing? Yes. You had a right to know, I get that. But surely you can forgive two people who did everything they could to give you a wonderful life? And surely you can forgive Elsie for being true to herself? Because that's what she did. She didn't try to be something she wasn't. She knew herself completely. Not many people have that knowledge. She knew your parents would give you things she possibly couldn't. She did that because she loved herself and she loved you. I think she deserves to be respected for being honest enough to do that.'

'You're taking her side?'

'It's not a matter of sides, Lottie. It's a matter of facts. And accepting life for what it is. It isn't always the fairy tale we all hope for. It isn't always what we want. But Elsie and your parents tried to make your life a fairy tale and now you think you hate them for it. You don't. You know you don't. And you don't hate Elsie either. I can see it in your eyes. Elsie loves you, Lottie. I could see that in her eyes last night. She loves you very much.'

'I ... I don't know what to do. I think I need to get away from here. To go back to Reading and think this through. But ... I love it here and I don't want to leave. I thought I'd found paradise, but I was wrong. I'm so confused.'

'You can't go anywhere in this weather. As for finding paradise, even paradise has problems. And it would break Elsie's heart if you left now. And not just Elsie's, Lottie. She might not be the only one in Seahorse Harbour who would feel like that.'

Twenty-Seven

There's not a lot you can say when you know someone is right.

And there's not a lot you can do when you love someone – other than tell them, or show them how you feel.

And loving someone isn't about that person being perfect, or living up to some expectation you have of them. It's about loving them, no matter what. About loving their faults and their good points. About accepting them for who they are and not trying to make them into what you want or expect them to be.

I didn't agree with what my mum and dad and Elsie had done, but after taking in everything Asher said, I began to see it from their point of view. If I desperately wanted a child and someone gave me the chance I thought I'd never have, perhaps I'd have done exactly what they did.

But I still needed more time to think this through. I'd lost a mum and come here to gain an aunt. Now I'd got a second chance at having a mum. And a mum who loved me. Perhaps not in the same way as my parents had, but in her own special way. Not many people got that chance.

I wanted family and I'd got it. I'd also made some new friends.

And more than that, I had found someone very special.

When Asher had said that Elsie might not be the only one in Seahorse Harbour who would feel heartbroken if I left, I assumed he was probably talking about Josie and Diana, but he looked into my eyes and I could see that he meant himself.

Suddenly, and without really thinking it through, I pulled him to me and kissed him on the lips.

At first the kiss was soft and tender but within seconds it had turned into a deep and passionate kiss, not just for me but for Asher too.

He wrapped his arms around me and pulled me even closer.

I was now perched on the edge of the sofa and the heat from the fire wasn't the only heat I was feeling. A much bigger and faster burning fire, took hold within me and before I knew what I was doing, I was tugging at Asher's shirt, desperate to touch him, to feel my hands on his skin, to press my body against his.

He clearly felt the same. He lifted my jumper over my head between kisses and unbuttoned the blouse beneath. His hand slid inside and cupped my breast and I heard myself gasp at the sheer thrill of his touch.

When I slid my hands over his chest and down his back, I felt him shudder with excitement and when I undid the button on his jeans and eased the zip down, he moaned my name so sexily that I almost had an orgasm on the spot.

He moved off the sofa and knelt on the floor in front of me, parting my knees gently and adeptly and pulling off my jeans as I wriggled out of them, all the while, kissing me.

Within a matter of seconds, his jeans and shirt were off and so were all my clothes. I was naked before him and I revelled in the look he was giving me. He wanted me as much as I wanted him, and that was even more evident as he struggled to pull off his boxers over his erection.

But it didn't take him long and as he surged into me, kissing me with such passion and intensity that my brain and body wanted to explode, I knew that I was about to have the best sex I had ever experienced.

And I was right. Oh, so right.

This man had skills. Many, many skills.

He knew exactly what to do to make me scream with pure pleasure and sob with complete joy. I had never had sex like this before. Every inch of my body tingled and ached and pulsated. I yearned for him to continue doing everything he was doing but I knew I couldn't hold back much longer.

I realised I didn't have to. Asher wanted me to let myself go, completely. And I did so more than once. I lost count of how many times I screamed with ecstasy. And I do mean ecstasy. This man was a god. A sex god.

I wanted him to feel as I was. To experience what I was experiencing. What I hadn't realised was that he was. I was so lost in my own blissful state that I hadn't recognised that he felt the same.

I'm not a sex goddess, by any means, but it seemed Asher thought I was. He moaned my name between urgent kisses. His body shuddered more than once and when we eventually lay on the carpet, wrapped in each other's arms, our mutual need finally satiated, he told me that he had never had sex like we'd just had.

The problem was, that thrilled me so much that I wanted to do it again.

He took my wandering hand in his and smiled at me, kissing me briefly on the lips.

'I may need a moment,' he said, his voice soft and husky and sexy as hell. But he was looking at me as if he wished he didn't. And then his smile widened and he rolled me onto my back. 'But just a moment, it seems. You clearly have super powers, Lottie Short.'

'I'm not the only one,' I said. 'You were unbelievable.'

'Unbelievable? Well then. I'd better make sure that this time, you believe it.'

Twenty-Eight

Luckily for us, not one person required Asher's services as a vet during the entire morning.

Or that afternoon.

Or that evening.

Not only had I never experienced sex like this, I'd never had so much sex in my life, let alone in one day.

We did take one or two breaks though. But only very short ones.

Asher gently coaxed me into sending Aunt Elsie a text and to telling her that I was with him. That was sometime during the morning. I kept it short and sweet and simply said that while I was still in shock, I was beginning to see why she and my parents did what they did and I wasn't quite so cross about it. I also said I'd see her later.

I also called Josie and told her where I was, but I didn't even finish the sentence.

'I know Elsie needs someone with her but—'

'Don't worry, Lottie. You take all the time you need. I'll stay here for now and Diana's here too. I hope you don't mind but Elsie and I both felt she had a right to know. And Merry's fine too. We're about to take her and Henry for a very short walk in the garden. We dare not venture far. Don't worry, we'll take good care of Merry. And Lottie. This means we're not cousins-in-law but real cousins. You do realise that don't you? Not that that matters really because we already think of you as family. But now you really are. In every sense of the word. So no matter what happens from here, you're stuck with me and Di. I just thought I'd mention that. Now go and have fun with Asher.'

Before I could say another word, she'd rung off.

I told Asher about it and he smiled.

'There you are. Another upside to your discovery. And I've made a discovery of my own. It seems I can't go for more than five minutes without kissing you.'

He pulled me close and did a whole lot more than kiss me.

We stopped for food at some point during the day and we had a shower in the afternoon. Although that also led to us having sex so that wasn't really a break.

We turned on the TV in Asher's bedroom, where we were spending the afternoon, so that we could see the news. Asher's parents and his sister were supposed to be coming to spend Christmas with him but the reports were dire.

The white-out had turned into a full-blown blizzard, which meant Asher's family couldn't get to Seahorse Harbour anytime soon, and neither could Josie and Diana's parents who were also coming for Christmas, I remembered.

All flights were grounded and all airports closed. Roads were blocked; entire villages were cut off. This was the worst blizzard in living memory and the reporters interviewed several people who moaned that this Christmas would be miserable.

I'd thought my Christmas would be miserable this year, but now I had a feeling this was going to be one of my best Christmases ever.

'Are you very disappointed that you won't be spending Christmas with your family?' I asked, snuggled up in Asher's arms.

'I would've been. If not for you. Now I don't think I'll mind anywhere near as much. But there's still a possibility they may be able to get through once this blizzard stops.'

'You're an optimist. I like that.'

'I'd like them to meet you. If they don't make it for Christmas, perhaps they might get here for New Year.'

'Ah. I'm only supposed to be staying for

one week. In theory, I'll have gone back to Reading by then.'

'But do you have to?'

The look on his face told me this wasn't just a holiday fling for him. And he could no doubt see the same on mine.

'I was actually thinking about staying for a while. But that was before today. Elsie had said I could stay with her. Now I'm not sure.'

He twisted my fingers through his and gave me a sheepish smile.

'You could stay here. If you really didn't want to return to Elsie's.'

'But not if your family arrives. And in any case, it wouldn't really work, would it?'

'Why not?'

His brows furrowed and he eased me away from him so that he could look me directly in the eye. I could see the doubt creeping in.

'Because your family might think it's odd to find a woman in your bed that they'd never heard of, for one thing. But more importantly, there's Merry.'

'Ah. Would it surprise you to know that they have heard of you? I told them about you when I spoke to them at breakfast this morning.'

'At breakfast? You told them about me? Why?'

He let out a small sigh and grinned.

'Because I liked you. A lot. And I had a

feeling you would become very important in my life. Don't ask me why, or how I knew. I just did. But what about Merry? Are you saying she wouldn't approve?'

I couldn't believe he'd already mentioned me to his family, but more to the point, I couldn't believe he thought I'd be important in his life. Was this love at first sight? I think it might've been for me. Could it be possible that it was the same for Asher?

'No. Not at all. I mean. She would definitely approve. She likes you. I can tell.'

'What's the issue then?'

'Have you seen your house?'

I glanced around the bedroom which was as pristine as everywhere else. This room had rich, deep purple walls and curtains only fractionally lighter. The floorboards were oak with a black stain over them and one deep purple rug. The ebony bed was a solid wood frame and the purple bedding looked and felt, expensive.

Asher looked around too.

'Er. What's the problem with my house? If it's the décor, that can be changed. But I can't see why Merry would worry about that.'

'I love the décor. And so would Merry. But have you ever owned a dog? Or had one come to stay? Your house is immaculate. After just one day you'd be finding dog hair everywhere.'

'I own a vacuum.' He laughed as he

relaxed. 'But the only reason my house is 'immaculate' as you call it is because I'm hardly ever here. I'm either in the surgery, on the beach, or at the sea life centre. Oh. Or in the pub. I will admit I like things tidy, but that's only because if they're not, I can never find anything. But if I had someone to come home to. And a dog to walk. I'd be spending a lot more time here. And you should see the place when Sorcha comes to stay. It looks as if a troupe of chimpanzees has had a rave and invited half the jungle. And contrary to what you might think, I rather like that.'

'Mess doesn't bother you then?'

'No. Mess doesn't bother me. But you do. You bother me a lot. Since that first moment I saw you in the village I haven't been able to stop thinking about you. I don't want to scare you off and I know we hardly know one another but I'm really hoping you'll stay in Seahorse Harbour, Lottie. If not with me then at least with someone. Although preferably not another man. You'll laugh at me when I tell you that I was worried you might be attracted to Kev and I thanked my lucky stars that he saw Lucy when he did.'

'Oh Asher.' I couldn't believe this. Not just what he was saying but the fact that he was saying it. 'I felt the same about you that night we met. I can't believe this is happening.'

He pulled me even closer.

'But you're glad it is, aren't you?'

'Absolutely. One hundred and ten per cent.'

'Good,' he said, emphatically. 'Because I think I've fallen in love with you. And although I'm surprised at how fast this is happening, I have to admit that I've never felt happier than I do today.'

Twenty-Nine

Asher had said that I had the most expressive eyes he'd ever seen. Well, I'd seen the expression in his eyes when he'd told me that he thought he loved me and I didn't have the slightest doubt that he did.

And I loved him. I knew it with every fibre of my being.

I'd heard about people falling in love at first sight but I had never expected it to happen to me.

But why shouldn't it? It can happen to anyone at any time.

That's the wonderful thing about Love. It's not something we can control. We can't set a date and say, right, I'll fall in love on that day. Equally, we can't stop it from happening. One day we might wake up feeling lost and lonely and doubting that we'll ever be in love again and suddenly – POW!

Someone comes along. Our eyes meet. And our whole world spins on its Axis. It only takes a minute. Not even that. And we somehow know that our life will never be the same again.

They say Christmas is a time for miracles and this Christmas was certainly producing a few of those.

Within a matter of days, I'd got a new family, new friends, a new and gorgeous boyfriend and the possibility of a new home, either with Asher or with Elsie.

I was being given a brand new start.

Positive thinking really worked. If I'd known that, I'd have tried it sooner.

I'd also been given another mum.

Instead of feeling cross and hurt and deceived, I needed to accept that I had been extremely lucky. Asher had made me realise that.

I'd had an idyllic childhood with parents who adored me.

My biological dad had died before my birth and there was nothing anyone could have done about that. I never got to meet him but I had a chance to learn about him now.

Elsie was my biological mum and whether I agreed with what she did or not, what was the point in raking over the past? In assigning blame, or bearing grudges. That would do no one any good. Least of all, me.

Now I had the chance to get to know her. To really know her. I already loved her. I knew that. And after talking about it all with Asher, I could see it so much more clearly now. He was right. We can't make those we love into what we want them to be. If we truly love them, we must accept who they are, warts and all.

'I'm going back to Elsie's,' I said, when Asher and I went downstairs for dinner. 'I'm supposed to be looking after her, and Josie and Diana have had to do that all day. But I wish I could stay here.'

He smiled. 'I'm glad, in a way. Not that you're going. My bed will feel empty tonight. But I think it's the right thing to do. For all concerned. And we'll have plenty of time to spend together once Elsie's injury has healed. Although I certainly hope you'll be coming back here at least once or day. Or that Elsie will let me come to you.'

'I'm sure she will. You're not getting rid of me that easily,' I joked.

'Getting rid of you is the last thing I want to do,' he said. 'I'll walk you back to Elsie's and we can tell her the matchmaking worked.'

I laughed. 'I think she probably knows that already. There was something in Josie's tone when we spoke earlier. As if she knew that you and I were doing a lot more than just talking.'

And I was right.

Elsie did know.

It took us a while to battle the elements and reach Elsie's cottage and we looked more like snowmen than humans when Josie opened the front door and let us in.

'You've come back,' I heard Elsie shout and I could hear the joy in her words as we shook off the masses of snow from our hats, coats and boots.

'I have,' I called back, as Merry came bounding into the hall to greet us, wagging her tail and throwing herself at our feet. She ended up with almost as much snow on her fur as we had on us.

Josie grinned at us.

'Had a good day?'

'Wonderful, thanks. I'm sorry for leaving you all day though.'

She waved a hand in the air.

'Think nothing of it. I know you may still be mad at her but Elsie is great company. And the abundance of alcohol in her hot chocolate, helps. Diana's here too and we've been catching up with everything.'

Asher and I walked towards the sitting room holding hands but before we entered the room Elsie said, 'Asher is welcome to come and spend the night whenever you like. Assuming that you're planning on staying here for a while that is.'

'Thanks, Elsie,' Asher said, grinning like a kid who had just been given the best Christmas present ever, and he kissed me on the lips in front of Elsie, Josie and Diana.

'I am,' I said. 'And thank you.'

'What for?' Elsie queried.

'For being you.'

'Oh', she said, with tears in her eyes and a catch in her voice. 'Does that mean you forgive me? I'm truly sorry if I hurt you, sweetheart. I hope you know that was the last thing I'd ever want to do.'

'I know. And yes. I do forgive you. But it may take some time for me to get used to this. I'm not even sure what to call you.'

'Call me anything you want to. You could still call me Elsie for now. The only people who know about this are in this room. It can stay that way if you like, but I know Josie and Diana might want to tell their families.'

'Of course,' I said, smiling at them both as Asher held my hand in his. 'And I'm happy for you to do that. Once I've had another day or so to adjust to it, I don't think I mind who knows, but I understand if you want to keep this all a secret, Elsie.'

'Me? I've been keeping this a secret for almost thirty-four years. I'd like to shout it from the rooftops now. But only if you're okay with that.'

I was more than a little relieved she felt that way. And also a little surprised.

'Don't you care what people might think?'

'I've never cared about that, sweetheart. At sixty-five, I'm not going to start worrying about it now.'

Josie laughed. 'Please let me be there when you tell Mum. Dad will take it in his stride but Mum will have a lot to say. Are you ready for that, Elsie?'

Elsie shook her head. 'Tibby always has a lot to say about everything. I rarely take any notice. I love her, of course, and I'm happy to take her grilling on this. She means well.'

'I need to call the hospital,' Diana said. 'The weather's getting even worse and there's no way I can get there and back tonight.'

'Diana!' Josie laughed. 'Don't you have anything to say on the subject?'

'Like what? Lottie's family now. But she was family yesterday. I've said all I had to say when you and Elsie told me. What more is there to say?' She glanced at me and smiled. 'Other than being astonished earlier by Elsie's revelation, this doesn't change that much as far as I'm concerned. It simply means we are actually blood relations. It doesn't change who we all are as people.'

'Thanks,' I said, unable to think of anything else.

'Do you mind if we get off?' Josie asked. 'I promised Orla we'd bake Christmas biscuits tonight.'

'Of course not,' I said. 'And feel free to tell them about all this. I'm sorry if I've messed up your day.'

'You haven't. It's been far more exciting

than I thought it would be when I got out of bed this morning. It just goes to show that no matter how well we think we know someone, we never really do.' She glanced at Elsie. 'Are there any other secrets you've been keeping?'

'Absolutely not. I can promise you that.'

'I'm not sure whether that's good or bad,' Diana said. 'The bit about us not really knowing someone. But it does mean that people can surprise us. I'm hoping Alex will surprise us all and stay faithful to me this time around.'

Josie tutted. 'You get more like Mum every day, Diana. You might want to watch that. Not everything is about you and Alex.'

'I know. Sorry. I can still be a bit selfish and self-centred, can't I? I need to work on that.'

'We'll work on it together,' Josie said. 'And now Lottie can help us too. Now let's leave Lottie and Elsie in peace. We'll see you all tomorrow.'

She smiled at us and at Asher as she dragged Diana into the hall, waving a cheery goodbye as she went.

'I'll be off too,' Asher said. 'But I'll call you later if that's okay?'

'You're welcome to stay,' Elsie said.

'Thanks. But I think you and Lottie need a bit of time alone. You must have a lot to discuss.'

I walked him to the front door and he shivered as he glanced outside. The snow was really coming down. If this kept up, we'd all be digging ourselves out. My car on the drive looked like a giant, white spaceship. A massive blob. And then I noticed that someone had etched a smiling face on the side of it. I had a feeling that was Josie.

'If you need anything, just call me,' Asher said, pulling me into his arms and kissing me goodbye.

'I need you,' I teased. 'I'll be thinking of you all night.'

'Ditto,' he replied. 'With bells on.'

Thirty

Elsie and I were awake for most of the night.

We talked for several hours in the sitting room and when I helped her upstairs to bed, it all felt different somehow.

I took up some hot chocolate and we sat in her bed, just as we had done the day before. Merry stretched out between us and within minutes, was snoring gently. But this time when Elsie wrapped an arm around my shoulder, I realised I was cuddling up to my mum, not my aunt, and it was the strangest feeling.

In a good way.

'What was Dad like? I hope you don't mind me asking.'

She looked at me and smiled.

'You can ask me anything, sweetheart. Absolutely anything. I promise to tell you the truth. Your dad was a wonderful man. He was very much like Lydia. I teased him that he was a clone of his big sister, and he agreed.' She laughed at the memory. 'I know I told you I didn't love him as much as I probably should have, but that doesn't mean I didn't love him a great deal. Because I did. And the strange thing is, even now, I miss him. Although, as I'm being honest, I think we would probably have been divorced by now. Not because of him. Because of me. I'm just not good at relationships. At least, I wasn't. My relationship with you is different. I may not have been good at that until now but it's something that's going to change. Having you here has been the best feeling in the world and I never want that to end.'

'You don't have any photos of him. Not even a wedding photo.'

I couldn't keep the sadness from my voice.

'Oh sweetheart, yes I do. I have hundreds of photos. They're in the attic in another trunk similar to the one in which you found your mum's letters.'

'My other mum.'

'Yes. Your other mum.'

'Why are they all in the attic?'

She sighed softly and hugged me tighter.

'Because although I come across as a free spirit and someone who doesn't care what anyone thinks, there are some things I care very deeply about. Eric was one of them. You are the other. If I had photos of Eric, I'd be reminded of the man I lost, every day of my life. And I'd also be reminded of you. I didn't want that. I don't believe in looking back. I have very happy memories and I don't need photos to remind me of those. Photos gather dust and there's something rather sad about them. At least that's what I think and how I feel. But if it'll make you happy to have a photo or two of your dad, then we'll get them out tomorrow and buy a frame and hang them on the wall.'

'I don't think photos are sad, but if you do then I don't want you to have them hanging on the wall. Perhaps I could have one by my bed?'

'Absolutely. You can have as many as you like.'

'If Dad had lived, would you have kept me?'

I could feel her body tense.

'Yes. But that doesn't mean I would've been a very good mother. In fact, I'm pretty sure I would've been terrible. Why don't we ask Asher to come and help you get the photos down tomorrow? We can invite him round for dinner and we can sit and go through the photos together. And then he can stay the night, if you like.'

She obviously didn't want to discuss what might have been. I suppose she was right not to. Neither of us could change the past so what was the point in dwelling on it. At least she had said she would've kept me and somehow that was a comfort.

I took a deep breath and grinned at her

over my hot chocolate.

'I'd like that very much. I've fallen for him in a big way.'

'I know you have. And the wonderful thing about that is it's clear he feels the same. I'm so pleased you decided to come to Seahorse Harbour, sweetheart. And now you have a reason to stay.'

'I have two reasons to stay. One is my budding relationship with Asher. The other is my growing relationship with you.'

She blinked several times as if she were holding back tears and she brushed my cheek with her fingers.

'Thank you, sweetheart. That means the world to me.'

We sat in silence for a while, drinking our hot chocolates, and something occurred to me.

'How do you feel about being a grandmother?'

Elsie nearly choked on her drink.

'Holy mopeds! A grandmother?' She laughed for a moment before giving me a tender and loving smile. 'You know what? I don't think I'd mind that at all. I have a feeling I'd make a better grandmother than a mother. But can I have a year or so to get used to the idea?'

Thirty-One

I don't know if the seahorses in Seahorse Harbour had called me to the village. But what I did know was that I was here to stay. I was absolutely certain of that.

Not that I could have left, even if I'd wanted to. Snow continued to fall, on and off, until Wednesday morning when it suddenly stopped and sunshine poured down from a bright, blue sky. But the village was effectively cut-off, together with numerous towns and villages throughout the UK.

One or two people trudged through the snow to get to Easterhill, and the local authority did the best they could to clear the roads or at least make them passable, but travelling anywhere other than a mile or so from your own front door, wasn't for the faint-hearted.

The police and all the motoring organisations advised people not to travel unless it was an emergency. Another weather front was moving in, according to the forecasts, and was likely to bring more snow with blizzard conditions once again. It was going to be a white Christmas. In every sense of the term.

Luckily, The General Store had ample provisions for the residents of the village and a good stock of tinned, frozen and ambient foods, together with all other household requirements.

Milk came from a local dairy farm situated between the village and Easterhill and thanks to the farmer's determination and his son's aptitude for business, fresh supplies reached the shelves of TGS every day and the doorsteps of many of the less able residents via a hastily set up milk delivery service.

Bev of Beach Bakers not only baked enough bread, rolls and cakes, along with all manner of festive fare such as chocolate logs, Christmas cakes and puddings, cinnamon rolls, mince pies and Christmas biscuits, for her own shelves but also sold stock to the store, meaning everyone was happy.

But when the snow began to melt on Wednesday, a collective sigh of relief went up amongst the shop keepers and many others. Even if the respite might only be brief.

The knowledge that more snow was to come brought grumbles and predictions of doom and gloom from several adults and gleeful squeals from most of the children and the young at heart, which included Elsie, Josie and Diana. Their delight at the prospect of heavy snow on Christmas Day was infectious and despite the difficulties involved in taking Merry for her daily walks, even I found myself excited at the thought.

Diana drove to the hospital and back a few times in Alex's Range Rover, which seemed able to cope with the conditions, and she was overjoyed to be told that he would be home before New Year, although sadly, not for Christmas.

Whether or not he had changed remained to be seen but from the things Diana told us, it did sound as if he had. Or that he was trying to change at the very least.

I finally met Mikkel Meloy on Wednesday, the day before Christmas Eve.

I'd spent almost the entire day on Tuesday going through Elsie's photos, along with Asher, Josie and Diana, whilst Liam worked at his pottery and Orla, Becca and Toby together with Orla's boyfriend, Darren, made the most of the snow, so I hadn't had a chance to catch up with Kev and George. I wanted to find out how things were going with Lucy, having received a text from Kev, late on Sunday night with just a thumbs up emoji, a smiley face and a couple of kisses.

I hadn't heard from him since and I'm ashamed to say that after my discovery on

Monday and spending the day with Asher, and then being busy all day on Tuesday, I hadn't texted to see how he was. Until Wednesday morning. We arranged to meet for a drink in The Seahorse Inn that evening.

The Seahorse Inn was warm and cosy and the atmosphere was welcoming, made more so by the roaring log fire in the large fireplace. The abundance of Christmas decorations also helped. A tall, fat pine tree stood in one corner, laden with lights and baubles in a multitude of colours. Twinkling lights were everywhere; entwined around the ropes and nets and other fishing paraphernalia hanging from the black beams and the low, white-washed ceiling; draped over the photographs of Seahorse Harbour through the ages, some sepia, some in colour, together with paintings of the sea, seahorses, or ships hanging on the walls. Lights were even wrapped around several ceramic seahorses and other items of Liam's pottery, on the deep and wide window sills. There were more lights behind the bar, and that's where I first saw Mikkel.

I could see why Diana had been reluctant to end their relationship. She'd told me he had Viking ancestry and that he was gorgeous and she had described him accurately.

'He's possibly every woman's dream-man,' she'd said. 'His smile can erase your memory, at least temporarily. His broad shoulders and

Emily Harvale

strong arms will keep you safe, no matter what. You'll long to run your hands through his mane of golden blond hair that curls at the ends as it brushes his shirt collar, and yearn to kiss his sensuous mouth. His eyes will make you melt, and so will his deep, rich voice, and his roar of laughter will have you laughing with him.'

'Er. Remind me again why you've dumped him?' Josie had said at the time.

I'd questioned her decision too.

'Are you sure you've made the right choice? Or is he just all good looks and no substance?'

'Oh no,' Diana had said. 'He has substance. He's kind and considerate. Intelligent and good at business but a fair and friendly boss, I believe. He's rich but he's generous with his wealth. Stylish in a casual way and not the least bit interested in designer labels. He's a good friend, especially when you really need one. And in bed, he's a god.'

'Wow!' I'd said. 'I didn't think men like that existed.'

But that was before I'd slept with Asher.

'Hello,' Mikkel said, when Asher introduced us. 'It's lovely to finally meet you. I've heard so many good things about you, Lottie and I can see all of them are true.'

He smiled at me and winked at Asher and Diana was right. That smile could erase your memory ... if you weren't already in love with someone like Asher.

278

'Thank you,' I said. 'I've heard good things about you too. And they're also true. I can see that.'

A crease momentarily formed between his dark golden brows as if he were wondering whether it had been Asher or someone else who'd mentioned him, but the smile soon returned and he looked me in the eye before leaning over the bar and saying hello to Merry.

The moment he did that, I knew I'd be friends with Mikkel Meloy. And I hoped he'd find someone special to take the place of Diana and fill the void she might have left in his heart.

'I hear you're planning to stay in Seahorse Harbour,' Mikkel said, darting a look at Asher while pouring the drinks Asher had ordered.

'Yes,' I said. 'I want to get to know my mum and my family. Not that I could leave in this weather, anyway.'

The smile faded a little.

'No. I love snow but this weather means my dad won't get over here from Norway, and that's a pity. I was looking forward to us spending Christmas together, especially now … my circumstances have changed. Oh. And I suppose that means your parents and Sorcha won't make it either, Asher?'

Asher shook his head. 'Sadly not. But the long-range forecast promises warmer weather in the run up to New Year's Eve, so they're intending to visit for the New Year celebrations instead.'

According to Asher, Seahorse Harbour put on quite a show for New Year. He'd already told me there were fireworks, a bonfire, and a BBQ on the beach on New Year's Eve, weather permitting. And a sponsored swim in the sea on New Year's morning which attracted a large crowd, apparently, and all the proceeds, naturally, went to save the seahorses.

He'd added that Lyn from the Seahorse Bites Café and Bev from Beach Bakers made special New Year's Day breakfasts, and provided free coffee, tea or hot chocolate to anyone brave enough to swim.

I wasn't quite sure how, but my name had suddenly appeared on the list of swimmers just hours after he had told me all about it. I wasn't looking forward to that although when Asher promised to warm me up afterwards, it began to have a certain appeal.

I was pleasantly surprised to see Kev had brought Lucy, especially as Asher was with me. Diana had kindly offered to stay with Elsie, so we had all evening to get acquainted.

Despite the things Josie and Orla had told me about Lucy, and the fact that her clothes made me feel as if mine had come from a jumble sale, I liked her. She asked questions but not too many, having heard the news about me and Elsie, along with everyone else in the village, and she didn't seem at all judgemental.

Not that anyone had, in truth. Not even Lilith, who I'd bumped into in Beach Bakers that morning and who'd said I must be thrilled to have a mum like Elsie. I told her I was, and left it at that.

'I won't tell a sole,' she said, tapping the tip of her nose with one finger, 'because, as you know, I'm not one to gossip.'

'We're happy for everyone to know,' I informed her with a friendly smile.

Although how the news had got out so fast, Elsie and I had no idea. Until Josie said that Orla may have mentioned it to Darren, who might have told his mum, who happened to know Doreen, Lilith's friend.

Another thing I liked about Lucy as the evening progressed, was that she seemed open and honest. She even told us that she'd behaved rather badly in the summer when she'd had a crush on Liam. That was a risky thing to admit in front of Kev but it didn't seem to faze him in the least and I think the three of us admired her for her honesty.

'I was a real bitch to Josie,' she said. 'And I tried to get in the way of Liam's happiness and I deeply regret that. My only excuse is that I hadn't lived in the village long and I was feeling really lonely.'

I knew exactly how that felt so I wouldn't condemn her for that.

'Liam's friendship was like a lifeline,' she

continued. 'But I clung to it far too tightly. I never seem to be able to make friends easily with women. I don't know why. I think I need to work on that.'

'Perhaps we can be friends,' I said.

She looked doubtful. 'What would Josie think about that?'

I smiled. 'I think if you tell Josie what you've just told us, she'll understand and give you a chance to start afresh. I don't know her or Diana well, obviously, but they don't seem the type to bear grudges for long. Especially not Josie.'

Lucy looked genuinely relieved. 'Thank you, Lottie. I'll do that.'

'And Christmas is the perfect time,' Kev said. 'It's all about forgiveness and new beginnings.'

'And the birth of baby Jesus,' I joked, repeating roughly what Reverend Perse had said at the Meet and Mingle Jingle.

'Ah yes,' Kev said, grinning.

'Excuse me for a moment,' Lucy said, smiling warmly. 'I need to go to the loo.'

Kev watched her go before leaning closer to me and Asher. 'Speaking of forgiveness, you'll never guess who I got a call from last night.'

'Your ex?' I said.

'Yep.'

'What did she say?' Asher asked. 'Did she

want you to take her back?'

Kev nodded.

'And?' I coaxed. 'What are you going to do?'

He sat up straight and his gaze wandered in the direction of the Ladies loo.

'I'm not going to take her back. I do still have feelings for her. We were together for two years and I can't just switch them off. But they're not burning as brightly as they were when I proposed. And I know it's early days, but I think Lucy and I are good together. You know how people say that the human race is like a broken jigsaw and we all have to find the bits that fit us perfectly?'

'No,' Asher said. 'I've never heard that.'

Kev grinned. 'Well I have. And it's as if Lucy and I are a perfect fit. The minute we saw one another, we just clicked. Okay, maybe not quite the minute she saw me, but as soon as I'd asked her to dance.'

'That I do agree with,' Asher said, turning to look me in the eye and taking my hand in his. 'I feel that way about Lottie.'

'And I feel the same about you,' I replied.

'You see,' Kev said. 'We're all part of the jigsaw. And it's coming together rather nicely.'

Thirty-Two

Just one week earlier, thanks to a Christmas card and a round Robin letter, I'd made a sudden decision to spend Christmas in Seahorse Harbour and to visit my aunt Elsie. I'd had no idea then how things would turn out. But never, in my wildest dreams could I have imagined any of this.

Merry and I were celebrating Christmas Eve with my mum, my new family including the kids, and my new boyfriend.

Snow was falling again, as the forecasters had predicted, but this evening, although the flakes were large, they fluttered down in the still night air. Not even the slightest breeze rustled the holly bushes in Elsie's garden, which, having only yesterday lost most of their covering of snow, were rapidly being blanketed in white once more.

The cottage was aglow, not only from the fairy lights strung all around but also from the fire and a number of battery-powered candles dotted here and there.

'I prefer the real thing,' Elsie said, as Asher and I switched on at least thirty of the realistic-looking candles. 'But you can't have naked flames on coffee tables when you've got two dogs in the house. Merry's tail may not quite reach high enough but Henry's definitely does.'

Josie, Diana, and their families, with the exception of Alex of course, were coming to Elsie's for a Christmas Eve buffet and, "enough alcohol to bring down Santa and his sleigh" – those were Elsie's words, not mine. Orla's boyfriend, Darren was joining us, but sadly not Becca's boyfriend, as he couldn't get here due to the weather and the fact his parents lived so far away.

When I told Elsie about Kev and Lucy, and what Lucy had said in the pub, she'd told me to text Kev and invite them too, including George.

'What about Josie and Liam? Won't they mind? It is supposed to be family, isn't it?'

'No,' Elsie said. 'Josie's not one to spoil a party, and neither's Liam. Besides, Josie may still moan about her sometimes, but deep down she forgave Lucy the minute Liam told Josie how much he loved her and that Lucy had never been anything more to him than just a friend. Not a very good friend, as it turned out. But we all have our good and bad days, and it does seem as if Lucy is trying to make amends.'

Elsie was right about Josie. She wasn't

thrilled to hear Lucy would be coming but when Lucy arrived and immediately handed Josie and Liam a Christmas card and a belated, 'moving in together' present and also apologised profusely for her behaviour, not just to them but to Orla, all was forgiven.

It was the perfect Christmas Eve. We played games, sang carols, ate and drank until none of us could eat or drink another thing, laughed until we cried, told ghost stories around the fire and finally, each opened one present from beneath the tree.

I cried when I opened a present from Elsie. It was a photo in a silver frame and it was of her with my dad Eric and my parents.

'That was taken just a month before Eric died,' she said.

The four of them stood in a line, the men at the ends and Elsie and my 'other' mum in the middle, and they all had their arms around each other. They were laughing, as if the photographer had told them a joke, but not so much as to spoil the photo. They looked as if they were having so much fun and it was clear that they all loved one another.

'It's such a beautiful photo,' I said, sobbing and smiling at the same time. 'All four of you look so happy.'

'We were, sweetheart. And it's not just the four of us in the photo. I didn't know it at the time, of course, but I was pregnant. Which means you're in the photo too. You may not be visible, but you're there.'

I couldn't help myself. I burst into tears yet again, but I dashed to Elsie's chair, and I hugged her so tight that I'm surprised she didn't snap in two.

'Thank you so, so much,' I sobbed.

'No, sweetheart. I'm the one who should be thanking you. I love you, Lottie. I love you with all of my heart.'

Tears were rolling down her cheeks as we looked at one another.

My mum and dad adored me and I adored them. Nothing would ever change that. I might not agree with the fact that they kept such a massive secret from me, but it didn't change the way I felt about them. I knew that. They'd raised me and they would always be my parents. But Eric was also my dad and Elsie was my mum too. And I loved them.

Instead of the bleak and lonely future I had expected for me and Merry, our futures were looking exceedingly bright and none of this would have happened if I hadn't come to Seahorse Harbour.

'Who could that be?' Diana said, as the doorbell rang out.

'Why not go and answer it and see?' Josie laughed.

'I'll go,' Becca said, getting to her feet.

A moment later, Becca shrieked with

excitement.

'Noah! You're here! You made it!'

Elsie brushed away her tears and beamed at me.

'That's Noah. Becca's boyfriend. We didn't think he'd get here.'

Becca and Noah came into the sitting room, their arms around each other. I wasn't surprised to see how handsome he was. Becca had described him to me and told me how they met. He was certainly tall, dark and dangerous looking, but from everything I'd heard, he was as soft as a kitten.

'How did you get here, Noah?' Diana asked, clearly impressed that he had.

'I borrowed Dad's car,' he said, as if that answered the question.

'But the roads are impassable in places,' she said.

A cheeky grin spread across his face.

'Yeah. But it's a Land Rover. And where there's a will there's a way, as Mum would say. I wanted to be here to see Becca on Christmas Eve and if that meant driving across a few fields on the way then that's what had to be done.'

'That's true love for you,' Josie said, glancing up at Liam. 'You'd drive across fields for me, wouldn't you?'

'Absolutely,' he said, kissing her on the lips.

Asher beamed at me and he didn't have to

say it.

I could see from the look in his eyes that he'd drive across fields for me.

People would do all sorts of things for Love. For True Love. And that sort of Love wasn't limited to lovers. True Love was the purest form of Love. It was selfless.

I might never quite understand how Elsie had been able to part with me, but what I did believe was that she did it because she loved me. And also because she loved my mum and dad.

But the past was the past and it was time I looked to the future.

With my new family and friends, with my mum, Elsie, with my beloved dog, Merry and with my boyfriend, Asher by my side, I was certain it was going to be a future filled with happiness and love.

And maybe, in the not too distant future, Elsie would become a grandmother.

That was something we could all look forward to.

Coming soon

I'll have exciting news about my new book coming very soon.

Check out my website for details or follow me on social media.

If you love my books, sign up for my newsletter, or join my exclusive, Facebook group. Details are on the next page. You'll be the first to hear all my news and you might even win a free gift in one of my regular giveaways.

A Note from Emily

Thank you for reading this book. If you loved it and want to be the first to find out about my new books, and also, chat with me and other fans, ask to join the exclusive Emily Harvale's Readers' Club Facebook group. Or go to: www.emilyharvale.com and subscribe to my newsletter via the 'Sign me up' box.

A little piece of my heart goes into all my books and when I send them on their way, I really hope they bring a smile to someone's face. If this book made you smile, or gave you a few pleasant hours of relaxation, I'd be delighted if you'd tell your friends.
I'd also love it if you have a minute or two to post a review. Just a few words will do, and a kind review makes such a difference to my day – to any author's day. Huge thanks to those of you who do so, and for your lovely comments and support on social media. Thank you.
A writer's life can be lonely at times. Sharing a virtual cup of coffee or a glass of wine, or exchanging a few friendly words on Facebook, Twitter or Instagram is so much fun.

I mentioned my newsletter just now. It's absolutely free, your email address is safe and won't be shared and I won't bombard you, I promise. You can enter competitions and enjoy some giveaways. In addition to that, there's my author page on Facebook and there's also my lovely, Facebook group. You can chat with me and with other fans and get access to my book news, snippets from my daily life, early extracts from my books and lots more besides. Details are on my website but you'll find all my contact links in the Contact section following this.

I'm working on my next book right now. Let's see where my characters take us this time. Hope to chat with you soon. In the meantime, I'm sending you love and virtual hugs. I can't wait to bring you more stories that I hope will capture your heart, mind and imagination, allowing you to escape into a world of romance in some enticingly beautiful settings.

To see details of my other books, please go to the books page on my website, or scan the QR code below to see all my books on Amazon.

Stay in touch with
Emily Harvale

If you want to be one of the first to hear Emily's news, find out about book releases, see covers, and enter free competitions, then sign up to her Readers' Club by visiting:

www.emilyharvale.com

and subscribing to her newsletter via the 'Sign me up' box. If you love Emily's books and want to chat with her and other fans, ask to join the exclusive

Emily Harvale's Readers' Club Facebook group

Or come and say 'Hello' on social media:

 @EmilyHarvaleWriter

 @EmilyHarvale

 @EmilyHarvale

Contact

If you want to be the first to hear Emily's news, find out about book releases, enter competitions and gain automatic entry into her Readers' Club, go to: www.emilyharvale.com and subscribe to her newsletter via the 'Sign me up' box. If you love Emily's books and want to chat with her and other fans, ask to join the exclusive Emily Harvale's Readers' Club Facebook group.

Or come and say 'Hello' on Facebook, Twitter and Instagram.

Contact Emily via social media:
www.twitter.com/emilyharvale
www.facebook.com/emilyharvalewriter
www.facebook.com/emilyharvale
www.instagram.com/emilyharvale

Or by email via the website:
www.emilyharvale.com

Acknowledgements

My grateful thanks go to the following:

Christina Harkness for her patience and care in editing this book.
My webmaster, David Cleworth who does so much more than website stuff.
My cover design team, JR.
Luke Brabants. Luke is a talented artist and can be found at: www.lukebrabants.com
My wonderful friends for their friendship and love. You know I love you all.
All the fabulous members of my Readers' Club. You help and support me in so many ways and I am truly grateful for your ongoing friendship. I wouldn't be where I am today without you.
My Twitter and Facebook friends, and fans of my Facebook author page. It's great to chat with you. You help to keep me (relatively) sane!

Printed in Great Britain
by Amazon